T0196017

MURDER IN THE WINE COUNTRY

"Kelly, would you like to join me this afternoon?" Gertie asked. "The club headquarters are in a garden given to the town by Esther Fallbrook when she passed. We maintain it and are given the use of a small cottage on the property. You might like to know about it to share with your guests."

"I'd be happy to meet you. I have an appointment with Phil and a group of his friends for a private wine tasting and discussion. I should be done by three and could meet you at three thirty. Will that work for you?"

"That will be fine."

"As you know, I'm trying to learn as much about the area as possible. Phil really wanted me to attend to hear a higher level of wine talk, as well as meet some of the local winery owners. He pointed out connections are always a good thing."

Gertie nodded. "He's right. This is about you becoming part of the community."

I loved hearing the words "becoming part of the community." I'd taken the job because everything about it was what I had longed for...my own niche in life, wonderful people to work with, and a small town setting.

"I'll see if we can get Rupert to join us and give us an update about the Succulent Saviors."

Gertie left, and my phone vibrated in my pocket. I took it out and saw a text from Phil.

The message read, **The police questioned me. The coroner's final report isn't in, but the blow that killed Eric clearly didn't come from the car accident. They think he was killed elsewhere and the crash was a cover-up. They are now considering it a murder investigation...**

Books by Janet Finsilver

MURDER AT REDWOOD COVE

MURDER AT THE MANSION

MURDER AT THE FORTUNE TELLER'S TABLE

MURDER AT THE MUSHROOM FESTIVAL

MURDER AT THE MARINA

MURDER IN THE WINE COUNTRY

Published by Kensington Publishing Corporation

Murder in the Wine Country

Janet Finsilver

LYRICAL UNDERGROUND
Kensington Publishing Corp.
www.kensingtonbooks.com

LYRICAL UNDERGROUND BOOKS are published by

Kensington Publishing Corp.
119 West 40th Street
New York, NY 10018

All Kensington titles, imprints, and distributed lines are available at special quantity discounts for bulk purchases for sales promotion, premiums, fund-raising, educational, or institutional use.

Special book excerpts or customized printings can also be created to fit specific needs. For details, write or phone the office of the Kensington Sales Manager: Kensington Publishing Corp., 119 West 40th Street, New York, NY 10018. Attn. Sales Department. Phone: 1-800-221-2647.

Lyrical Underground and Lyrical Underground logo Reg. US Pat. & TM Off.

First Electronic Edition: April 2020
ISBN-13: 978-1-5161-0426-0 (ebook)
ISBN-10: 1-5161-0426-9 (ebook)

First Print Edition: April 2020
ISBN-13: 978-1-5161-0427-7
ISBN-10: 1-5161-0427-7

Printed in the United States of America

To E.J., my husband, who encouraged me on this journey as a mystery writer.

ACKNOWLEDGMENTS

I am grateful to my husband, E.J., who is always willing to give me feedback and help me find answers to questions. My great critique group made up of Colleen Casey, Staci McLaughlin, Ann Parker, Carole Price, and Penny Warner gave me valuable feedback and are cherished friends. I want to give a special thanks to Bob Becker, Certified Sommelier and Certified Wine Educator, who taught me a lot about wine and answered my many questions. I'm very fortunate to have a great agent, Dawn Dowdle, and a wonderful editor, John Scognamiglio. Thank you all for being there for me.

Chapter 1

I opened the door to the lounge of the Redwood Cove Community Center and froze. Miniature baby goats filled the room. Some balanced on top of the couches, three frolicked in front of the fireplace, and others bounced on the chairs. A black and white spotted one standing on top of a coffee table snacked on a bouquet of yellow daisies.

Scott Thompson, manager of the center, was yelling, "Shoo...out...go" as he waved his hands at the little creatures.

All he got in return were a few bleats. None of them moved in the direction he wanted them to go, which was toward the back door.

I joined in and grabbed a blanket a cream-colored goat had pulled off a rocking chair. A tug-of-war ensued, which I lost as I landed on my stomach. Before I could get up, a brown goat began tap dancing on my back. I sat up, and he slid off. A tiny white one plopped into my lap.

I began to laugh and soon tears cascaded down my cheeks. How could I not? Scott, a city boy in the country, now turned goat wrangler, sat down abruptly on a couch and joined me in laughing at the hilarious scene. The black and white spotted one on the table made a leap and landed next to him, a yellow flower dangling from its mouth. A black spot on its forehead resembled a heart.

A heavyset man I didn't recognize rushed into the room. "Sparky, get down," he yelled at the goat next to Scott.

Sparky wiggled his ears but didn't move.

"I'm so sorry about this," the man said. "I'm Bruce Kincaid, and these are the Nigerian Dwarf goats you wanted to rent for the yoga class. I couldn't get my rig close enough to the livestock pens, so I put them in the backyard temporarily until I could move them. I was coming around to the front door to tell you." He looked around at the herd, which was in constant motion. "Clearly I wasn't fast enough."

Scott wiped the tears from his face with the back of his hand. "Not a problem. I can't remember the last time I laughed so much or so hard." He stood. "I didn't realize they were there and opened the back door to let in some fresh air."

"Point me in the direction you want them to go, and I'll get them back in the yard," the goat owner said.

Two border collies had entered with the man and crouched at his side, their eyes intently watching the goats.

"There's a sliding glass door in the meeting room adjacent to this lounge." Scott walked to a door in the corner of the room. "I'll go open it."

He returned a few moments later. "You're all set."

The man gave a sharp whistle and called out, "Tim, Sally," and pointed to the door Scott had left open. The dogs leaped into action one going to the left, the other right. The goats paid attention. In seconds, a herd was formed and began to move in the direction Bruce indicated.

Suddenly, Sparky made a break for it, but Sally was faster and cut him off. The miniature goat made a pirouette and rejoined his friends. After lots of kicking, bleating, and head butting, the four-legged intruders eventually disappeared headed for the backyard.

I got off the floor and looked at Scott. "Goat yoga?"

He raised one eyebrow at me. "Sure. It's the latest craze. Haven't you heard?"

I shook my head. "Seriously?"

Scott nodded. "I had the same reaction when members of the center's planning committee brought it up. People say the goats bring a different level of experience to yoga as well as an opportunity for lots of laughter... which we certainly got to experience. Participants say they leave the classes happier and more relaxed then they have felt in a long time."

"Bruce said you were renting them."

"Right. We decided to see how it goes before investing in our own herd. If it's successful, we'll buy our own goats. If we do, some of the veterans want to explore making goat cheese."

Michael Corrigan, our mutual boss and owner of Resorts International, built the center to benefit the residents of the isolated community of Redwood Cove, located on the northern California coast, by providing services and classes to help promote a healthy lifestyle. In addition, there were many struggling veterans in the area, some of them homeless. Cabins had been built to house the ex-military on-site.

I noticed the time on the grandfather clock in the corner and saw it was close to eight. "We'd better get to the barn. The meeting is about to start."

Michael had invited some of the wealthiest philanthropists in the country to attend an event at the center, hoping they would be encouraged to replicate this community support model elsewhere. Guests would be staying at Resorts International properties. I managed Redwood Cove Bed and Breakfast, an inn owned by Michael, and would be helping out during the occasion.

We went outside and headed for the recently completed barn-sized structure on the property. The name of Redwood Cove Community Meeting Facility had been shortened to "the barn" in everyday communication. Michael had wanted to build something large enough to accommodate big community events. The recent addition to the property had already been the site of a Russian formal ballroom and would now be used for the meeting with the "movers and shakers," as Michael called them.

The community center was about ten miles inland from the Pacific Coast. The fog had burned off and the sun shone through the towering redwood trees. The walkway had verdant green pastures on the right side. The resident llamas watched as we approached then walked next to us until the fence stopped them. I figured they were hoping for treats, which I often supplied, or a quick scratch under the chin. No time for it today.

The doors to the meeting area were wide open, and we walked in. Rows of chairs were set up, and we chose a couple of empty ones at the back. Notepads and pens were on each seat, along with a packet of information. We picked those up as we sat.

Daniel Stevens, manager of a sister property called the Ridley House, was a few rows up. He saw us sit and waved. His long, straight, black ponytail, high cheekbones, and light copper skin left no doubt of his Native American heritage.

I surveyed the room and saw several other managers as well as some veterans who lived on-site. The center employed a number of locals to run the place, and they made up the rest of the group.

Michael Corrigan stood at a lectern at the front of the room. The faded blue jeans and denim shirt gave no hint of his billionaire status. He looked more like a large lumberjack than an internationally known top player in the financial world. He had a heart of gold and considered his employees family. Help was there whenever they needed it.

I opened the notepad and uncapped the pen. Michael had been sending updates as planning for the event progressed. Today we'd hear about everything that was scheduled.

Michael said, "Welcome, everyone. Thank you for coming. We have a lot to discuss. Please take the papers out of your packet and look them over."

I did as requested and found schedules for the guests as well as a pamphlet with color photos and descriptions of plants and other information. Today was Monday. Thursday was the official start of the event, and he'd welcome his guests at a wine and cheese reception in the evening.

Friday, members of the community and the veterans would talk about what the community center had done for them. The veterans would demonstrate the training they'd been doing with Post Traumatic Stress Disorder service dogs. That evening there'd be a barbecue.

The main event would be a gourmet food and wine tasting experience on Saturday. The guests would have an opportunity to mingle with locals and veterans in an informal setting.

"As some of you know, it's been a dream of mine to have others do something similar to what I've created here so more people can benefit. My purpose is to explain what we've done, have members of the community share what changes this has brought to their lives, and have the veterans living here tell their stories."

I'd seen the changes in the veterans' lives, and I'd heard the buzz in the community over the opportunities the center provided for them. I hoped Michael would be successful.

"I think the schedules are self-explanatory," Michael said. "I asked a number of local chefs to be part of the Saturday event, and they were happy to do it."

Scott nudged my arm. I turned toward him.

He whispered in my ear, "I volunteered."

I wasn't surprised. He was a superb cook and enjoyed any opportunity to try new recipes.

Michael continued, "I invited my guests to bring a chef to participate if they were interested. Many of them have private chefs and some own restaurants." He chuckled. "The idea was wildly successful, and many wanted to participate."

Michael shared that most of the chefs were arriving today so they could get used to their cooking areas. They had permission to use the kitchens at the inns where they were staying, as well as the community center's two kitchens, one located in the meeting building and the other in the main house.

"Chefs will be foraging for local wild edible plants tomorrow and Wednesday. Three wineries have volunteered their properties for the hunt, and we will host a group here at the community center. Half of the chefs will forage at two sites tomorrow morning while others will be working in their assigned kitchens. Everyone will have lunch here then swap roles. The same plan will be used on Wednesday. I worked with a botanist, and she developed the pamphlet of edible wild plants in your packet."

I looked at the long list of plants. I was surprised at how many were listed. The woman had done an excellent job supplying photos as well as descriptions. A picture of fireweed caught my eye with its colorful purple stalks of flowers.

"I'd like to introduce Warden Luis Rodriguez of the California Department of Fish and Wildlife. He wants to discuss a problem that has been happening in the area."

Luis took Michael's place at the podium. He wore a tan uniform with an official name tag on the right side. A bright blue Fish and Wildlife emblem was on his left sleeve. The light glinted off his wavy dark hair.

"I want you to know there has been plant poaching going on of a succulent called Dudleya farinosa. It, unfortunately, has become a popular plant as a status symbol of Chinese middle-class families. The plants sell for about fifty dollars each. State wardens recently discovered the poaching operation is much larger than we thought. Literally tons of them have been picked. A photo of one is in your packet."

I leafed through the pages until I found the picture. The plant's thick pale green leaves formed a rosette pattern. A note said that the color could range from what was in the photo to having tips of bright colors, especially red.

Plant poaching? Who knew?

"I'm going to strongly suggest anyone foraging search in teams. Nothing violent has happened yet, but a lot of money is involved. You need to be careful and attentive to what is happening around you. The plants grow primarily on rocky seaside cliffs and coastal hillsides."

I raised my hand, and he nodded at me. "What makes this particular plant so sought after?"

"Tending succulents has become a favorite pastime in China, and the Dudleya farinosa has become particularly desirable because it's hard to obtain." He looked around the room. "Any other questions?"

No one raised a hand, so Luis picked up his notes and moved away from the lectern.

Michael stepped forward. "Thank you, Luis."

"You're welcome," the warden replied.

"He'll meet with the people hunting tomorrow and share this news with them." Michael continued, "The guests returned forms with personal information to help make their stay as pleasant as possible as well as let us know of any concerns they might have. Managers of the inns where they will be staying have received copies."

Deputy Bill Stanton entered the room and sat next to Scott. I wondered what he was doing here.

Michael nodded in his direction. "One of our guests has a stalker and two have received threats around some projects they are involved in. That's not unusual for people with their kind of wealth and influence. A number of them have bodyguards and will be bringing them."

He shared that surveillance cameras had been installed and explained the veterans would take turns patrolling the property. He and Deputy Stanton had met several times to discuss the role local law enforcement would play.

"Deputy Stanton and I are reviewing the plans today after the meeting. Does anyone have any questions?"

Everyone shook their head.

"The theme for the event is The West: Past and Present. The dress is casual clothing, Western style is encouraged. The people attending have mostly formal occasions in their life. I want this to be relaxed and fun. If you feel like getting into costume as someone from the days of the Old West, feel free to do so."

It sounded like an opportunity to wear my ranch clothes from home— cowboy boots and a Stetson hat.

"That's it then," Michael said. "Managers, packets with copies of the information you just received have been delivered to your inns to distribute to attendees and staff. Our next meeting is tomorrow morning at eight to welcome our chefs."

We'd gone from learning about fun activities to hearing about plant poaching and being cautioned to be careful. We were ending with news of a stalker and threats. The course of the day had taken a dark turn.

Chapter 2

On that somber note, Scott and I headed back to the main building.

"That sure wasn't how I imagined the meeting would end," I said.

Scott nodded. "I knew about the issues because I handled the surveillance equipment installation."

We entered the room where the goats had frolicked. I spied Phil, full name Philopoimen Xanthis, wine expert extraordinaire, sitting at a table with a young redheaded man. I wondered if he had been teased like I had growing up with red hair. Scott and I joined them.

"Kelly and Scott, so good to see you both. I'd like you to meet a friend of mine, Eric Stapleton," Phil said.

He introduced us and then said, "We're preparing a wine tasting class for Michael's event. Please join us and sample some wine."

"I'll have to pass," Scott said. "But thanks for the invitation. I have to meet with one of the new veterans about his cabin."

He bid us farewell and left. Phil pulled a chair out for me, and I sat next to him. He provided the wine for many of the inns in the area, including mine, and stayed at Redwood Cove Bed and Breakfast when he was in town.

Small vials covered the table, along with several bottles of wine and numerous glasses. I picked up one of the little jars labeled jasmine.

Eric smiled. "Take the top off, sniff, and see what you think."

I did as he suggested and was rewarded with the flower's sweet scent.

Phil pushed several vials in my direction. "We will use these during the class to teach people what smells they can detect in a variety of wines. Everyone's sense of taste and smell is different, and these scents help people learn that."

"Fascinating." I proceeded to check out several other jars.

"These are Eric's," Phil said. "He teaches classes on a regular basis. We're working together on this one."

I put one labeled eucalyptus back on the table after enjoying its refreshing scent, which reminded me of mint with a hint of honey. "Eric, I created themed rooms at the inn, and one of them involves wine tasting opportunities in the area. The scents along with directions would make a delightful addition to the Wine Room. Could I hire you to put that together for me?"

"Sure. It sounds like fun. I won't be able to do it for a while, though. I'm in charge of choosing vendors for an upcoming fundraiser for a local hospital. I'm also acting as a consultant for the sale of the Sagatini Winery."

I took out a business card and handed it to him. "I look forward to hearing from you."

Phil shook his head. "I hate to see another family-owned business disappear."

I hadn't been in the area long and wasn't familiar with this winery, but I'd heard Phil bemoan the loss of other small wineries.

"Carlo's ready to retire and his son, Lorenzo, doesn't want to carry on. It's a tough business, and if you don't love it, it's not the place to be." Eric tightened the lids on his jars. "Thanks for offering to look over the paperwork I've put together. I appreciate having a knowledgeable wine person examine the data to see if I missed anything."

"Happy to help," Phil said. "What's Lorenzo going to do?"

Eric started to gather his vials and put them in a box. "He and some of his friends have put together a real estate venture."

Phil helped him with the jars. "I'm guessing Carlo is disappointed."

"That's my guess as well. But...Lorenzo is ready for a change. I can understand that." He turned to me. "Nice to meet you, Ms. Jackson."

"Please call me Kelly. I look forward to hearing from you."

Just then a young woman came in carrying a full grocery bag with celery stalks and a narrow baguette sticking out of the top. "Hi! I'm Cassie MacGregor," she announced with a wide smile. "I was pointed in this direction to use the kitchen."

Her cropped hair was as black as Daniel's, with his Native American lineage, but the creamy white complexion spoke of a different heritage. Irish I would guess. Dark red lipstick emphasized her light skin.

I stood. "I'll show you where it is."

Suddenly the overloaded bag split and groceries spilled to the floor. Cans rolled under couches and chairs. Miraculously, a quart of milk stayed intact. We all began gathering the items.

"I'll get some bags from the kitchen," I said

I returned a few moments later. Cassie and Eric reached for the baguette at the same time, grabbing it at each end.

They laughed and Cassie said, "You can have it. You win."

At that moment, a man with the same color hair as Cassie's, along with a full beard, came in. He scowled at Eric, came over to where they were, and knelt down. I put the bags next to the food. He grabbed one and began shoving items into it.

The smile left Cassie's face. "This is my husband, Ian."

"Howdy." He didn't look up from what he was doing.

We stood when all the food had been picked up.

Before I could make introductions, Ian said, "Cas, where's the kitchen?"

I pointed to the door behind me. "I was about to show her when the bag broke."

Ian grabbed the other bags, picked up the one he'd filled, and walked toward the kitchen.

Cassie's lips trembled, and I thought she was about to cry.

Wanting to break the tense moment, I put out my hand. "I'm Kelly Jackson, manager of Redwood Cove Bed and Breakfast. Nice to meet you."

Cassie shook my hand, and a hint of a smile appeared.

Phil put out his hand as well. "I'm Phil Xanthis and this is my friend Eric Stapleton."

By the time Cassie had shaken Phil's hand and Eric's, her composure had returned.

"Nice to meet you all," she said. "Will you all be attending the events?" We nodded.

"Terrific. I'll see you around then. Thanks for your help." She smiled, the trembling gone. "Now it's time for me to get to work."

She left, and Phil and I helped Eric finish packing his supplies.

"I'll take these to the barn where we'll be holding the class." He turned to me. "I'll be in touch." Then he left.

Phil picked up his notebook. "I have some deliveries to make then I'll be back at the inn. I have a new wine I'd like you to try."

"Okay, but as you know, I trust you to make the decisions. You're the expert."

"I appreciate your trust, Kelly. However, I think it's important to continue to hone your skills. Many people come here because of the wine produced in this region. Being able to discuss wine with your guests would be helpful."

"I completely agree. You've already taught me a lot." I smiled at him. "See you in a bit."

He whistled a tune as he left, did a quick twirl, and gave me a wave goodbye. Phil loved Greek dancing and occasionally delighted the locals by performing on the spur of the moment when a musical group played one of his favorite tunes.

I went to the rocking chair and straightened the cashmere throw that had provided the tug of war between me and the goat, then headed for the kitchen to get some treats for the llamas. I reached out to grab the door handle then stopped.

"I saw the way you were looking at him. You were flirting," Ian's angry voice boomed.

"No, I wasn't." Cassie's voice sounded ready to break. "Ian, your jealousy is out of hand." Her voice had gone up a notch, taking on a shrill quality.

I turned to go. The llamas would have to do without this time. I left the building and walked to my Jeep.

As I drove back to the inn, I thought about what was ahead for the rest of the day. I had read the guests' forms as I soon as I received them. Julie Simmons, one of the chefs, arrived today with her service dog, Rex, a seizure alert dog.

I had decided to put her in the Cook's Room. Decorating it had been fun. I received a lot of help from the Silver Sentinels, a crime-solving group of seniors I worked with from time to time. They scoured thrift shops and garage sales, searching for items to add to the themed décor.

The room now had handmade potholders from Portugal in the shape of owls, an impressive collection of trivets from all over the world, and some antique cookie cutters. And, of course, lots of cookbooks. I had put up a notecard that said we'd be happy to run off twenty recipes at no charge.

I turned off the road and into the inn's driveway. I never tired of admiring the vines of colorful flowers that wound their way up the walls of the white building. Built in the eighteen nineties, the eaves on the home had the intricate gingerbread trim that was so popular in that era.

I parked in back and noticed a Subaru station wagon with an Oregon license plate in the visitors' parking area with a young woman inside. As I closed the door of my Jeep, she got out and walked over, followed by a cattle dog wearing a blue service vest. His coloring reminded me of a roan horse with his red and white hairs intermingling. Most of his face was a solid rusty red color.

The woman had large, deep brown eyes and long brown hair with blond highlights. She smiled, revealing even rows of white teeth a model would envy.

"Hi. I'm Julie Simmons." She looked down at her companion. "And this is my dog, Rex."

Rex wagged his tail but stayed at Julie's side.

"I'm Kelly Jackson, the manager of the inn. I love dogs. May I pet him?"

"Sure."

I petted his head. "I grew up on a Wyoming ranch. We always had several dogs, and one looked a lot like Rex." I straightened up. "Come on inside, and we'll get you registered."

"Good news! I know I'm really early. That's why I was staying in the car. I didn't want to bother anyone."

"If the room's ready, we're happy to check you in now."

I led her up the back steps and into the main work area, where the kitchen was located. I knew she'd been assigned ours for her cooking. A black granite counter separated it from the rest of the room and served as a casual eating area. The large wooden table to the left provided a dining area for more formal occasions and a worktable when necessary.

Helen, an inn employee, was working at the sink and turned as we entered. Her brown hair had slight streaks of gray at the temples.

"Hi, Helen, this is Julie Simmons." I turned to Julie. "I'd like you to meet Helen Rogers, amazing baker and highly organized, efficient assistant."

Helen blushed at the compliments. "Thanks, Kelly, you're sweet."

"Happy to meet you," Julie said. "I hope we have time to talk cooking. Baking isn't my strongest area, and I'm sure there's a lot I can learn from you."

"I'd love to chat with you. I know you're a chef, and I'm sure I can learn a lot from you as well."

I inclined my head toward the front of the inn. "Follow me, and we'll get you signed in."

"Your room is ready," Helen said. "We put a dog bed and bowls in there as well."

We proceeded to the front of the inn, passing the parlor as we went. I told Julie about the wine and cheese from four to seven. The flames from the burning logs in the fireplace danced lazily from side to side. I pointed out the local information on the coffee table.

Julie filled out the guest sheet. "I'd like to talk with you about my seizures so you know what to do if I have one. Rex usually alerts me well enough in advance that I have time to prepare myself. I haven't had one for a long time. That's why I'm allowed to drive."

"How does Rex alert you?"

"He paws my knee." Julie reached down and scratched him behind his right ear. "What I need when I have a seizure is a safe place to lie down on my side. Because my arms and legs thrash, it's important that hard or sharp objects aren't nearby."

The beautiful young woman spoke in a matter-of-fact tone. It was clear she accepted that seizures were a part of her life and did what she needed to do to deal with them.

"Thanks for telling me," I said. "I'll pass it on to the other employees."

"I appreciate it." Julie pulled a manila envelope out of her purse. She frowned and paused. "My family is in Bend, Oregon, where I work. Here's contact information for them. Kelly, would you be willing to look after Rex if something happened to me until they could come and get him?"

"Of course."

The frown disappeared. "Thank you so much. I don't expect to have any problems, but I like to cover my bases, and I'd hate to have him put in a kennel or the pound."

I nodded. "I understand."

She pulled a piece of paper from the envelope. "This is a letter I created for situations like this."

Julie picked up a pen from the counter and put my name on a blank line at the top and signed the bottom.

She handed the paper and the envelope to me. "This gives you guardianship over him and has all the instructions you need for feeding him. Copies of his vaccinations and license are in the envelope as well."

"Thanks. You're certainly thorough."

We went back to the kitchen area, and I put Julie's information on the counter. I'd put it in the safe later. Helen was preparing the cheese platters for the evening appetizers.

Just as I started to point out where equipment was kept in the kitchen, the back door burst open. Tommy, Helen's son, came running in with his basset hound, Fred, on his heels. I knew it was a minimum day at school because it was all he had talked about at breakfast.

"Mom! Mom!" he shouted.

"Tommy, lower your voice."

"Sorry." He shot a quick glance at Julie and me. He bounced up and down on the balls of his feet, the energy from his voice now channeled into his body. "My project won the science fair. I got first place! First place!"

Helen gave him a big hug. "That's wonderful, honey."

Tommy had really turned a corner as far as his life in Redwood Cove was concerned. When I first met him, he had hated it here. He had a touch of Asperger's, and social skills were a challenge for him. Kids at school tormented him. With the help of Allie, Daniel Steven's daughter, and friends he'd made in math and science clubs, that had all changed.

"I can't wait to tell Deputy Stanton. He helped me with it, so he won, too."

Helen was a widower and lived in a cottage on-site. Deputy Stanton had stepped in to help Tommy with school projects.

Fred padded over to Rex, where he sat at Julie's side, and they touched noses. Tails began to wag. Fred went into play pose with his front down and his rear up. Rex didn't do the same.

"My name's Julie," she said to Tommy. "And this is Rex. What's your dog's name?"

"Fred." Tommy sat at the counter to eat the snack his mother had put out for him.

"It looks like he wants to play. Rex can only play when I give him permission. We'll definitely make some time for the two dogs to get together."

"Fred would like that," Tommy replied. "He's always ready to have a good time."

"May I give him a cookie?" Julie asked.

Tommy nodded enthusiastically. "You bet. He loves treats."

Julie pulled a blue cloth bag with the emblem of a running dog on its side out of her pocket, removed two cookies, and held them up for us to see. They were heart-shaped and had an "R" in the middle.

"I bake these for Rex. They're his special treat. I made the mold." She shrugged her shoulders and smiled. "I'm a chef. What can I say?"

She gave each dog a cookie and said goodbye to Helen and Tommy. I took Julie and Rex to her room.

She tilted her head as she read the title on the door. "Cook's Room?"

"Right. We have themed rooms at the inn. Helen and I thought you'd enjoy this one."

Julie oohed and aahed as she made her way around the room. When she got to the cookbooks, she looked at me. "I may never leave this room."

"I'm glad you like it. Can I help you bring in your luggage?"

"No thanks. I'm traveling light."

Rex settled on the dog bed, clearly knowing where he belonged.

"Okay. I'll see you later," I said.

The rest of the afternoon and evening went smoothly. Phil had me taste the new wine and work on my "enobabble," as I now knew "wine talk" was called. The term came from combining enology, the study of wine, and babble, to talk in a meaningless way. He explained some people got carried away using descriptors like stalky, racy, and wet river rock.

He invited me to a special wine tasting event he was doing for some local vintners. I agreed, knowing it would further my education and provide an opportunity for me to meet people in the area.

I looked forward to tomorrow with foraging, wine tasting, and visiting chefs on the menu.

* * * *

The next morning, I prepared a breakfast basket to take to the building where Phil stayed. It was a separate unit with four rooms and a common area on the second floor. As I turned to go, I saw Phil's face in the backdoor window. His skin had a gray pallor to it.

I waved him in. "Phil, are you okay?"

He shook his head. "No."

"What's wrong?"

"Eric's dead."

Chapter 3

"Oh, no!" I reached out and touched Phil's arm. "What happened?"

He ran his hand over his face. "Eric was in a car accident on the way home. His pickup went off the road."

"Come in and sit down." I gently pulled him toward the worktable.

He shook his head as he sat. "I can't believe it…don't want to believe it. Such a nice young man with a bright future ahead."

"Would you like some coffee?" I asked.

"Sure."

I'd poured him coffee numerous times and knew he liked it black. Helen came in as I handed the cup to Phil. She'd left our breakfast preparations to wake Tommy. She glanced at Phil, frowned, and looked at me with raised eyebrows.

"Phil just learned one of his friends was killed in an automobile accident last night."

"Oh, Phil, I'm so sorry to hear that," Helen said.

"Thanks," he replied.

"The baskets are ready to go," I said to Helen. "I want to spend a few minutes with Phil, then I'll help you deliver them."

"I can handle taking them to the rooms." Phil had his back to her, and she nodded in his direction.

I got the unspoken message to stay with Phil.

"Okay. I appreciate it." I retrieved my mug from the counter and took a chair next to Phil. "Did you know Eric well?"

"Fairly well. He wasn't a close friend, but we've known each other for about five years. He was a wine person, like me, and we attended a lot of events together and enjoyed talking wine. Very likeable. Always a ready smile." He sipped his coffee. "I think having worked with him yesterday and now finding out he's dead makes the shock worse."

"I can understand." I felt the strangeness of it myself as images of Eric laughing as he helped Cassie pick up groceries flashed through my mind.

"Well," he said wearily. "I have work to do."

He stood and seemed to have aged with his slow movements and slumped shoulders.

"I was getting ready to bring you breakfast."

"I can take it, though I don't know how much I'll eat."

I retrieved the basket and handed it to him. "I understand."

I watched through the window as he walked back to his room with heavy steps.

With him gone, I could help with the deliveries. I saw two baskets left, and one of them was Julie's. I dropped the first one off, knocked lightly on the door, and headed for the Cook's Room. As I put the breakfast on the floor and raised my hand to knock, Julie opened the door.

"Good morning." She flashed one of her beautiful smiles. "I was getting ready to take Rex for a walk."

He was on his leash at her side.

I picked up the basket. "I can put this on your table in your room if you'd like."

"Sure." She opened the door wider. "I had a great time looking through the cookbooks. I'm definitely going to take you up on copying recipes."

"I'm glad you enjoyed them." I put the basket on a small table. "Did you get a chance to look at today's schedule?"

"I did. It looks like fun. I plan on going to both of the foraging excursions this morning."

I exited the room. "I'm going to do the first one myself so I can see what it's all about. A cook I'm not, but I love learning new things."

"I'll see you at the meeting then." She stepped into the hallway and closed her door.

"You can put the basket outside your room when you're done."

"Okay."

I returned to the kitchen, where Helen and I cleaned up the remains of the breakfast preparation and started the rounds of picking up the baskets that were finished and doing the dishes. She put Tommy's breakfast parfait, as I called it, on the counter. The attractive layers of all organic granola, yogurt, strawberries, and blueberries made a colorful, as well as nutritious, start to his day.

The door swung open as if on cue and he bounded in, his ever-present four-legged companion following closely behind.

"Good morning, Miss Kelly."

We'd decided he would call me that. It was an easy combination of formal and informal. I taught school for a short period of time, and that was what the students liked to call me.

"Hi, Tommy." I looked at the hound. "And good morning to you, Fred."

His thick tail wagged, and he grinned.

Tommy filled Fred's dish with kibble then settled on a stool and began to eat.

"Miss Kelly, do you have any jobs I can do for you to earn some money? There's something I want to buy for Fred."

His mom frowned. "Tommy, I told you not to pester people for work."

"It's all right, Helen." I looked at Tommy. "I'll think about it. What is it you want to get?"

"It's a camera that lets me watch Fred and talk to him when I'm not here. And I can even give him treats with it. I figured I could say hi to him and feed him during my lunchtime at school."

"That sounds intriguing. I've never heard of anything like that."

"It's called a Furbo."

"I'm sure I'll be able to come up with something for you to do."

"Oh, boy! Thanks."

Julie came in with her basket. "Helen, those muffins were incredible. The sweet orange smell made my mouth water before I even tasted one. Will you share your recipe with me?"

"Of course. I'm glad you liked them."

"They're one of my favorites." I pointed to a plate with the remaining crumbs of one I'd had for breakfast.

Tommy slid off the stool. "Gotta go."

He gave Fred a hug and grabbed his backpack loaded with his schoolbooks.

"Tommy," Helen said, "remember you and Allie and I are going to the craft store for project supplies. Be thinking about what you'll need."

"I have been. I started a list. I explained it to Deputy Stanton, and he said he'd be happy to help me. I'll text him and see if he has any ideas about what I should get."

Helen tousled his blond hair then gave him a hug. "Time to get going."

With his quick-moving style, he sprinted out the door. A moment later, he pedaled by the side window, his bike moving from side to side as he picked up speed.

Julie laughed. "He's certainly a bundle of energy."

"That he is," Helen said.

Julie turned to me. "I'll see you at the meeting."

She and Rex went out the back door.

"It sounds like there are some Bill Stanton breakfasts in the near future," I commented.

Helen had a ritual of fixing the officer breakfast as a thank you for helping Tommy. Bill was single and his interests didn't include cooking. His job kept him on the go. He welcomed Helen's home-cooked food, and I knew it had nourished him through some long days.

"I'm going on the first foraging expedition to see what that's all about," I said. "It might be something I can add to our guest book."

"I read the list of activities," Helen said. "Michael's put together an informative and fun few days for people."

I nodded and agreed. "It's a well thought-out combination."

I went to my room and grabbed a heavy navy fleece to ward off the chill of the coastal air. I filled the jacket's ample pockets with what I needed from my purse and put on hiking boots for the morning's walk through the woods. I picked up the plant information from yesterday's meeting, folded it, and put it in my back pocket.

I drove to the community center to meet the chefs and learn about the details of the day. I parked next to a Volkswagen Beetle, got out, and circled the car, admiring the colorful artwork painted on it. The bright lime green car was covered with garlands of flowers winding over the sides. A big daisy covered the roof.

I took several photographs with my phone. My mom and sister would get a kick out of the "flower" car.

Cassie came out of the main building and waved. "How do you like my car?"

"I love it. It must lift your spirits every time you see it."

She joined me. "It does…and it brings a smile to the faces of lots of other people as well."

"I can imagine. Are you going foraging?"

"Indeed I am."

We walked toward the meeting area. "Are you feeling comfortable in the building's kitchen?"

"Yes. I'll be sharing it with Scott Thompson. We've already worked out a schedule."

If her husband was jealous about Eric, wait until he met Scott with his six-foot-plus height, dark hair, and blue eyes.

We arrived at the barn. Julie and Rex were on the end of the last row. She glanced in our direction then jumped up and rushed over to Cassie and gave her a big hug. "It's so terrific to see you. I heard you'd be here."

Cassie reciprocated with an equally enthusiastic embrace. "It's been too long."

Julie said to me, "We've known each other for years. We went to cooking school together."

"Good morning, everyone," Michael said, and we quickly took our seats.

I did a head count and came up with twenty-seven people in the room. Most of them were the guests' chefs, as well as the local ones.

"Thank you all for coming and planning to participate in our food event here at the center on Saturday. I'm sure the day will bring delicious food, superb wines, and an opportunity for a good time."

The group nodded enthusiastically.

"I'd like everyone to introduce themselves and state where you live and where you work."

Everyone did so. They were from all over the country, with the exception of five local chefs.

Michael thanked them. "You should have received the event schedules for the week and a description of the plants you'll be looking for today. Directions to the wineries that are hosting the foraging parties and a map of their properties were included."

I saw the warden from yesterday approach Michael.

Michael moved away from the podium. "I want to introduce Warden Luis Rodriguez. He's here to tell you about a problem we've been having in the area."

"Thank you, Michael." He addressed the group and proceeded to explain the plant poaching as he had done yesterday.

"The poaching has occurred on both private and public land. No one has been hurt yet. However, there is a lot of money involved...and the poachers don't want to get caught. Please be vigilant. I highly recommend you forage with at least one other person. We don't want there to be a first-time problem. Violence and money often come hand in hand."

He emphasized the words "at least." These poachers were breaking the law...and he was right about violence and money.

Misgivings began to push out the anticipation of a fun morning.

Chapter 4

Cassie sat between Julie and me. She leaned toward Julie and whispered loud enough for me to hear, "Do you want to be my partner?"

"Sure," Julie replied.

Cassie then turned to me. "Are you going foraging?"

"I was planning on it."

"Do you want to come with us?"

"I would love to. Thanks for asking me."

The warden stepped down and Michael was again at the lectern. "The first group of foragers will meet at the Sagatini Winery in half an hour. You'll be introduced to the owners and will be able to ask any questions you might have. After foraging for an hour, we'll get together and see what people have discovered. There'll be refreshments available."

He went on to tell us the same scenario would take place at the next location, with lunch for everyone back at the barn when they returned. This would give the first group of plant pickers a chance to share with the chefs who had been cooking. The foragers would discuss their finds and talk about ways they might use them in their cooking. "All the information is on your chef's schedule along with your group assignments and cooking sites."

Michael informed us canvas bags for our hunts were on the table next to the door.

He adjourned the meeting, and we all stood. I noticed Scott on the far side of the room standing next to an enormous man with an enormous dog, a black and white Great Dane, at his side. Thoughts of Paul Bunyan and Babe the Blue Ox went through my head.

"I want to say hi to Scott, then I'll head out and meet you at the winery."

"Okay," Cassie said.

The two young women walked away, talking as fast as they could, catching up on each other's lives.

I joined Scott and the Paul Bunyan look-alike.

"Hi, Kelly. I'd like you to meet a new resident of the community center." He turned to the man next to him. "This is Garl Hancock and his dog, Toby. Garl, this is Kelly Jackson, manager of Redwood Cove Bed and Breakfast."

"Nice to meet you." He held out his hand.

Mine completely disappeared from sight as we shook.

"Like wise," I said. "Garl. That's an unusual name."

"Yep. I'm probably the one and only. Named after my grandpappy. Family figured there was probably a mistake on his birth certificate. Hey, if it was good enough for him his entire life, it's good enough for me."

I turned to the harlequin Great Dane.

Garl said, "Toby, shake."

The next thing I knew, I was holding a very large paw in my hand.

I laughed. "Nice to meet you, Toby."

The dog wagged his tail in reply.

"I've never seen a dog this big."

"He's my Post Traumatic Stress Disorder service dog, PTSD for short. I'm a big guy, figured I needed a big dog."

I could repeat the word big again when describing these two.

"He wakes me up at night if I'm having nightmares and helps in other ways."

Our conversation was interrupted by a black and white speed demon I knew to be Sparky the goat. He raced up to Toby and butted him in the side. The dog looked startled, but he didn't move.

Garl knelt next to the baby goat and scratched his head. "Hey there, little fella."

Sparky's light blue eyes with dark rectangular pupils stared up at Garl.

Jim Patterson, who managed the animals and the garden, came trotting in.

"This guy is a real escape artist. All the others are in the pen content to climb the trees and eat the bushes in their yard. This one? No. It's his second time out today."

Garl stood, grabbed Sparky before he could bolt, and tucked him under his arm. "Show me where he belongs, and I'll take him back for you. We had some of these little critters on the family farm when I was growing up."

"Thanks for the help. Follow me."

Garl towered over Jim, who wasn't a small man by any means. I heard them exchange names and noticed Garl continued to scratch Sparky's head. A gentle giant, for sure. Toby ambled after him.

I turned to Scott. "I'm foraging with a couple of the chefs. I need to get going." I raised an eyebrow at him. "If I find anything edible, do you want me to bring it back for you to use?"

"Sure, if you'll help me prepare whatever you find."

"You are a brave man, given my cooking skills."

My last cooking fiasco, in the form of a lesson from Scott, ended in a flour-covered kitchen as well as a flour-covered Scott.

"I don't think there's much you could do in the disaster category with a bunch of greens."

"Don't be too sure."

We shared a laugh, and I departed. When I reached my Jeep, I checked the directions to Sagatini's. I remembered the winery was the one Phil and Eric talked about yesterday. Eric's smiling face entered my mind, and I shook my head at the thought of him being dead. How quickly life could be over.

I joined the chefs at the winery as the hosts, Carlo and Lorenzo Sagatini, introduced themselves. There was no mistaking father and son, the family resemblance was so strong. Carlo wore black-framed glasses and a tailored black suit. His silver hair was brushed back from his forehead. Lorenzo had the same head of thick hair, but his was still primarily black. Only a few silver hairs had made their appearance.

We were seated outside at long tables covered with white cloths and decorated with lavish flower displays. Signs pointed to a tasting room and shop across from us that had large glass windows. Those windows provided guests with views of a gently rolling landscape filled with vines. At the top of a hill in front of us, I saw what looked like an Italian villa. Its tan coloring had a golden hue. Olive-green shutters framed the windows.

After answering a few questions, Carlo and Lorenzo wished us luck. The map showed a couple places we could drive to, or we could walk, taking one of the numerous paths from the winery.

"Let's walk," Cassie said. "It'll feel good after all the traveling time to get here yesterday."

"Good idea," Julie said. "I noticed on the maps of the other sites you have to drive to the different areas. This is the only one with paths right from the main building." She turned to me. "Does that work for you?"

I nodded. "Absolutely."

"Let's take a path that leads toward the ocean. Maybe we'll get some good views," Cassie said.

We pulled out our plant guides and did a quick survey of the pictures. Julie folded her papers. "I'm ready if you all are."

Cassie and I nodded in agreement, and we walked to the nearest path headed for the Pacific. Majestic redwoods lined our way.

Cassie stopped after a couple of minutes and looked at the photo sheet. Then she bent down and compared one of the pictures to a plant. "It's Queen's Cup, and there's plenty of it for all of us to take some."

She picked a few handfuls and stuffed them in her bag then moved aside. Julie and I followed suit. The attractive plant had smooth leaves like an orchid and a small white flower.

Cassie nibbled on a leaf. "The description says the leaves have a mild, sweet taste. I agree. They'll make a nice addition to a salad, and we have flowers for decorations as well."

We walked, talked, plucked, and picked. We had quite a haul after only twenty minutes. We had chickweed, wild mint, mustard, and pigweed to name a few.

Cassie tore off a piece of pigweed, chewed it, and made a face. "From now on, I'll believe the notes when they say something is bitter!"

I peered into my bag. "I had no idea there were so many wild edibles."

"Back in the Appalachian Mountains, where I grew up, people looked forward to the spring for picking ramps, a wild onion with a short growing season," Cassie said.

We came around a bend and caught a glimpse of the bright blue Pacific Ocean and stopped to admire it. The sunlight glinting off the water and the spewing white foam of the waves was something I never tired of seeing.

Then I began to get a funny feeling…like someone was watching me. My brothers and I used to see if we could get people to look at us by staring at them. It was our way to see if people could feel our stares… and it worked almost every time. The person's head would suddenly turn in our direction. Then Mom found out what we were doing, and that was the end of that. However, it convinced me you often could know when someone was watching you.

I shifted uneasily and glanced at Cassie and Julie to see if they seemed to notice anything. They were telling "remember when" stories and laughing. This area was similar to what the warden described as being where Dudleya farinosa could be found…and possibly the poachers.

A rock cliff had replaced the tall trees, and bushes lined one side of the path. I glanced over my shoulder but didn't see anyone. Then I thought I spotted some movement in the shrubs. My heart began to beat faster. Time to leave.

I turned to the two friends. "We'd better head back. There's less than half an hour left."

Julie petted Rex. "Right. Thanks for keeping track of the time. We've been so busy talking, I didn't think to check."

We turned and I peered at the bushes we had to pass on our way back, where I thought I'd seen something. Suddenly, a heavyset, dark-haired man stepped out and blocked our path. Another man and a woman joined him. They formed a line across the trail.

It was clear they weren't going to let us pass.

Chapter 5

My breathing quickened as adrenaline pumped through my body.

The first man took a step toward us.

We took a step back.

"What do you have in those bags?" His tone was curt, his voice loud.

Rex growled and his hackles rose. The dog moved toward him. The man retreated.

The three wore yellow vests and all had binoculars and cameras. Seeing what they were carrying, my anxiety began to lessen. People out to do you harm usually didn't sport that kind of equipment. Anger began to push out the fear.

"You're blocking our path. Please move," I retorted.

"Who are you?" Cassie asked.

The woman, petite with gray hair, straightened her shoulders and stretched herself upward to be as tall as possible. "I'm Prudence Sweeney, and we are the Succulent Saviors."

Succulent Saviors?

"Who?" Julie asked in a bewildered tone.

"We're an organization dedicated to stopping the poaching of the Dudleya farinosa."

A laugh of relief wanted to come out, but I tamped it back down. Not a good idea.

"I'm Rupert Pence," said the third person. "President of the Succulent Saviors. Now, what have you been picking?"

His worn tan dungarees stopped a couple of inches above sturdy brown leather sandals. Thick straps wrapped around his bulky white socks. Wispy strands of gray hair stuck out above his ears, and his bald pate glistened in the morning sun.

I opened my bag and walked up to them. "We've been collecting wild edibles. These two women are chefs and are part of an event that's taking place at the Redwood Cove Community Center."

"I'm Bert Wagner," the first man said as he peered into my bag.

I handed it to him. "Here. Look for yourself."

He rummaged around then handed it back to me. "I apologize for startling you."

"Same here," Rupert said. "The poaching has been going on for some time. The plants take years to grow, and they're being ripped up and taken out by the truckloads. We're trying to help catch the thieves."

I hoisted the bag onto my shoulder. "The warden told us about the thefts and warned us to be careful."

Rupert nodded. "We don't know of anyone being assaulted as yet, but that doesn't mean it won't happen. That's why we watch in teams of three or four."

Cassie nodded. "We were advised to search with others as well."

"We'll be going now," Prudence said. "Sorry to have bothered you."

"Easy to see how you might have thought we were up to no good," Julie said.

They walked by us headed toward the barren cliff areas, where the plants were likely to be.

We picked up our pace to get back on time. Cassie and Julie talked about what we'd found and how they would prepare the plants. Boil and stir were terms I knew. When they mentioned chiffonade and meunière, I had no clue what they were talking about.

"I thought I'd make a sauce with some of the greens and nap chicken breasts with it," Cassie said.

I could tell this had nothing to do with getting some sleep.

"Good idea about napping the chicken. Covering them with an herb sauce should be attractive as well as tasty," Julie said. "I did some research before coming. Many of the recipes suggested cooking the wild edibles for long periods, so I brought a tagine."

I was good with context clues and figured nap meant to cover and guessed a tagine was a piece of equipment.

Curious as to exactly what it was, I asked, "What is a tagine?"

"It's a Moroccan dish used for slow cooking, usually made of clay. Their use in north African countries dates back centuries."

I smiled. "I have my new word for the day."

When we arrived at our starting point, we found tables set with ornate silver urns of coffee and water for tea as well as an array of pastries. I helped myself to a chocolate croissant and poured a cup of coffee. Give me strong, black French roast with chocolate in a flaky pastry and I had two of my favorite flavors.

In addition to the usual muffins and pastries, the Sagatinis had put out traditional Italian sweets with placards giving the names and the basic ingredients. I walked along, reading the different types. A cannoli, a tube of fried pastry with a sweet ricotta cheese filling, made its way onto my plate. A bruttiboni, an almond-flavored biscuit, found a place next to it.

Small bins had been stacked off to one side and each labeled with a chef's name. The foragers could put what they'd found in them and clear their sacks for the next round. Michael, being his usual super-organized self, even had one made for me. The containers would be taken to the barn and made available when the chefs ate lunch. I finished my snack, thanked Cassie and Julie for the wild edible education, and said goodbye.

I wasn't attending the lunch, so I retrieved my bin, put my plants in it, and loaded it in my Jeep. I drove back to the inn, put the greens in the refrigerator, and went to the study.

After a couple of hours preparing food and wine orders and paying bills, I headed for the conference room. I glanced at the plaque with the name Silver Sentinels Conference Room over the door. I knew the group of crime-solving senior citizens was meeting today. The word "silver" reflected the color of their hair.

The Professor, as he liked to be called, had emailed reminders. In his scholarly life as a professor at the University of California at Berkeley, he'd been known as Herbert Winthrop. His tweed jackets and wool caps fit his title to a T.

I opened the door to the room and found Gertrude Plumber putting out chart paper. Short in size but strong in character, she was a force to be reckoned with. She'd made it clear the name Gertrude was not to be used. She was Gertie, thank you very much.

"Perfect timing," I said. "I'll put a couple of those up on the wall."

"Hi, Kelly. I'll get the felt pens out while you do that."

Helen had put out coffee, tea, and water. Mary Rutledge, another member of the group, would arrive with something sweet to eat. Her penchant for baking benefitted all of us. I pulled the tiny dog bed from the closet, as Mary would be bringing her four-legged kid—Princess the Chihuahua. I wondered what bejeweled collar color she'd be wearing today.

The Doblinsky brothers rounded out the players. Husky Ivan and slender Rudy were a contrast—rough and shaggy for one brother and refined and neatly trimmed for the other. Ivan's booming voice heralded their arrival.

Mary showed up right behind them, pink dog purse over one shoulder, personal purse over the other, and a plastic container in her hands. "Hello, everyone." Her soft voice sounded slightly out of breath.

I took the box and put it on the table.

"I made butterscotch pecan cookies. Kelly, please take the lid off while I take care of Princess."

"Happy to." The sweet sugary scent of freshly baked cookies wafted into the air.

Mary opened the dog carrier and Princess popped up. Dark green diamond-shaped stones studded her collar, and she wore a matching fuzzy dog coat. Mary picked the little dog up and put her on the floor. After the tan Chihuahua made the rounds greeting everyone, she curled up in her bed.

The Professor arrived and the group was complete. He wore his tweed hat at a jaunty angle and unbuttoned his sports coat as he entered. "It's a bit nippy out there today."

I remembered my first trip to the area. The ocean air mixed with fog sent a chill deep inside me. My Wyoming down jacket came with me when I moved here. We had plenty of sunny days and mild weather, but there were cold ones as well. Many tourists were caught off guard by the California coastal weather.

Gertie put ballpoint pens on the table. "It's a couple of minutes before noon. Everyone please get settled so we can start our weekly meeting on time."

Once a schoolteacher, always a schoolteacher. Gertie kept the group in line and on time.

After everyone seated themselves, Gertie picked up her gavel and rapped the table. "Welcome, everyone. We aren't currently working on any cases, so the purpose of today's meeting is to decide on our next project as well as discuss our presentations for Michael's event."

They took a few minutes to review what they would talk about Friday. Michael had asked them to tell what the community center had done for the residents of Redwood Cove. I enjoyed listening to them share how the classes had improved the lives of many friends and neighbors. I hoped Michael would succeed at convincing others to create something similar.

Mary nudged her cookie container resting in the center of the table with a plump finger. "One of my mother's recipes I haven't made in ages. They were among my favorites growing up." She looked around at the group. "On to our next project. What crimes do we know about that are happening in Redwood Cove?"

"There's the usual pickpocketing and petty store thefts," the Professor said.

Rudy stood, took one of the marking pens, and wrote the Professor's comments.

"Car break-in at grocery last night," Ivan said, his Russian accent giving the event a more melodramatic edge than perhaps the act deserved.

I piped up, "At the community center meeting yesterday, a warden talked about the plant poaching that's been taking place and suggested there was a potential for violence. He went so far as to say we should search in teams when we went foraging for plants, one of the activities that's taking place."

Gertie nodded. "My plant club is all roiled up about it. Some of them have made a subgroup called the Succulent Saviors and are patrolling the areas where the thefts have been happening."

"I met some of them today," I said.

I explained about the foraging, where I had been, and who I had met.

"Rupert created the Succulent Saviors and organizes the search parties," Gertie said.

I frowned. "Gertie, what's so special about these plants? And why the passionate reactions?"

"They take a long time to grow. Some of the most coveted ones take decades to mature. Their loss is creating an adverse reaction in our ecosystem…and the plants belong to the people of California. It's not right their numbers are being decimated."

"Well, then," the Professor said, "it seems the poaching is an area to explore. With the amount of emotion it's generating and the possibility of danger, it's impacting our community which is what we've joined together to protect."

Rudy started a new paper with plant poachers at the top.

"Our club has gathered a lot of material about the thefts," Gertie said. "I can bring copies of what we've learned to our next meeting. I'll check with Rupert as well to see what exactly the Succulent Saviors are doing."

Ivan finished the last of the cookie he'd been eating. "When do we want to meet next?"

"I can get the information this afternoon," Gertie said.

The Professor twirled his pen. "I think we should seriously take this on after what Kelly has shared. I'd like to meet tomorrow at the same time. Is everyone available?"

People nodded in the affirmative. I checked the meeting room schedule and assured them the room was available. Gertie banged her gavel, and the meeting ended.

I put the dirty dishes on a tray, as the group, except for Gertie, bid us farewell and departed.

Gertie began gathering the pens. "Kelly, would you like to join me this afternoon? The club headquarters are in a garden given to the town by Esther Fallbrook when she passed. We maintain it and are given the use of a small cottage on the property. You might like to know about it to share with your guests."

"I'd be happy to meet you. I have an appointment with Phil and a group of his friends for a private wine tasting and discussion. I should be done by three and could meet you at three thirty. Will that work for you?"

"That will be fine."

"As you know, I'm trying to learn as much about the area as possible. Phil really wanted me to attend to hear a higher level of wine talk, as well as meet some of the local winery owners. He pointed out connections are always a good thing."

Gertie nodded. "He's right. This is about you becoming part of the community."

I loved hearing the words "becoming part of the community." I'd taken the job because everything about it was what I had longed for...my own niche in life, wonderful people to work with, and a small town setting.

"I'll see if we can get Rupert to join us and give us an update about the Succulent Saviors."

Gertie left, and my phone vibrated in my pocket. I took it out and saw a text from Phil.

The message read, **The police questioned me. The coroner's final report isn't in, but the blow that killed Eric clearly didn't come from the car accident. They think he was killed elsewhere and the crash was a cover-up. They are now considering it a murder investigation.**

My stomach turned. Eric murdered? Why?

Chapter 6

I called Phil.

He answered after one ring. "Kelly, thanks for calling. I…I really wanted to talk to you…share what I know…"

I understood where Phil was coming from. Sometimes talking about a situation helped to reduce the stress.

"What happened?"

Phil sighed. "Deputy Stanton saw me yesterday with Eric. He thought I might be able to tell him something helpful, so he called to set up a time to meet then came by to question me."

"Why have they decided Eric wasn't killed in the accident?"

"The blow that killed him was on the back of his head, close to the top. There was nothing in his vehicle that could have hit him at that spot. His truck went down a hill and Eric was found slumped over the steering wheel at the bottom with his seat belt on."

"It sounds like the police are on the right track about it not being an accident." I frowned. "Were you able to tell him anything that would help the investigation?"

"Maybe. Eric told me he was going home to work on the hospital event and the winery sale. They found him at Drake's Cove, which isn't on the way to where he lives. Stanton asked about any problems Eric might have had with someone, but I couldn't help him there."

"Maybe they'll be able to turn up something about why Eric was in that area."

"I hope so," Phil said.

"Are you still planning your event for this afternoon?"

"Yes. There's nothing more I can do to help the police. I told Deputy Stanton I had some of Eric's wine tasting equipment, and he said he'd let the family know. Continuing to work is the best thing for me now."

"I know what you mean. I'll be there."

We ended the call. I picked up the tray and the dishes rattled as my hands trembled. It had been a shock to learn Eric was killed, but being murdered took it to another level. While the Silver Sentinels and I weren't strangers to dealing with murder cases, it was still hard to reckon with the fact someone had taken another's life…and a killer was on the loose.

I agreed with Phil about work being the answer. I paused. That and letting the Sentinels know. Their eyes and ears could be gathering information. I put the tray down and texted the group.

After putting the dishes in the dishwasher, I went to my quarters and fixed a cheddar cheese sandwich. I knew Julie had the use of the inn's kitchen from one to five. I didn't have to leave for half an hour and wanted to be available to answer any questions she might have. I took my lunch and headed for the work area.

Julie had placed a large pot on the stove and was rummaging through a drawer. A tall young man with a shock of blond hair that reminded me of Tommy's was busy chopping celery on a wooden cutting board. The wrinkles around his eyes belied his youthful appearance. He looked vaguely familiar. Rex had found a place to curl up out of the way, but where he could still see Julie.

"Perfect timing," she said as I entered the room. "Where do you keep soup ladles?"

I rarely cooked in the inn's kitchen…of course, I rarely cooked at all… but as the manager, I felt it important to become familiar with what we had and where it was kept. I put down my sandwich and showed Julie the drawers on the opposite of the counter.

She pulled out a steel ladle with a curved handle. "Thanks. This is perfect."

The young man waved at me. "I'm Sebastian Reynolds. I'd shake hands, but you'd end up with celery juice on you."

"I'm Kelly Jackson, the manager here. Nice to meet you."

"Same here. I'm being Julie's sous chef today." He looked at her. "Thank you again for letting me work with you."

"I'm the one who should be thanking you. Lucky me. I'm certainly not going to turn down an offer of free help."

Sebastian grinned and went back to chopping.

I sat on a stool and picked up my sandwich. "Sebastian, I feel like I've seen you before."

"I'm one of the veterans living at the Redwood Cove Community Center. We've never formally met, but I've seen you there. Once I was putting out hay for the llamas on the far side of the pasture when you were feeding them treats. They clearly chose your carrots over the dry grass I was offering."

I laughed. "I wouldn't take it personally."

"I won't," he replied. "I'm sure I'd make the same choice."

Julie placed a frying pan on a burner, put some oil in it, turned on the heat, and then removed a paper bundle from the refrigerator. "Sebastian, I'm curious as to why you wanted to help."

"I want to become a chef, like you," he replied. "This is an opportunity for me to learn from one of the best."

Julie blushed a bit. "Thanks for the compliment. Have you done much cooking?"

"In the army…though maybe that's not what you mean when you ask about cooking. I worked in the mess hall part of the time."

She laughed as she opened the parcel and put chunks of cut-up meat that looked like beef in the frying pan. It sizzled as it hit the heated oil. "Anything other than that?"

"I've worked part-time at some of the restaurants in the area, and I've been studying a lot." He winked at her. "Are you going to make a mirepoix with these chopped vegetables?"

"Whoa! Mirepoix. I'm impressed." She stirred the meat.

"And I'm confused," I said.

Sebastian scraped the celery into a bowl and started on a stack of peeled carrots. "It's a mixture of carrots, celery, and onions that's cooked slowly and used as a base for sauces, soups, and other foods."

"Right you are," Julie said. "Though, that's not what we're doing with them today. I thought with the theme of The West: Past and Present, it would be fun to make chili, a staple of early settlers, using the wild edibles I found and putting a twist on it by adding dark chocolate, which is all the rage these days."

Sebastian glanced at her. "Julie, when I heard about the theme a few months ago, I bought some sourdough starter called Skookumchuck that's supposed to be over a hundred years old. I began making bread." He frowned and hesitated. "I don't want to intrude on what you had planned, but I'd be happy to make some loaves to go with the chili."

She turned down the burner. "That'll make a perfect combination. Thanks for the offer."

"I find kneading the dough very relaxing, and there's nothing that smells better to me than baking bread. I've also become very popular at the center with all the loaves I've given out."

"I'll bet you have," Julie said. "I know you have to keep feeding the starter to keep it alive."

He nodded and said ruefully, "Yeah. The starter has become sort of like family now. I named it Mildred and feed her every other day."

We all laughed, and I glanced at the clock on the wall. Time for me to go. "I need to leave. Helen's number is on the wall next to the phone if you have a question. She's next door in her cottage."

"Got it," Julie said. "Thanks for your help."

I took my empty plate back to my room. The brief interlude had pushed Eric's murder out of my mind, but now it returned in force. I checked my phone. All of the Sentinels had replied sharing their shock and concern. As they went about their day, they'd be looking and listening for anything that might lead to an answer about what happened to Eric.

I shrugged into a heavy fleece, retrieved my purse, and took my foraging finds out of the refrigerator and left. I parked in front of the main building and carried my box of wild edibles inside. The kitchen was empty. I felt a pang of disappointment. I had envisioned seeing Scott with his dancing blue eyes and wide smile. I put the greens in the refrigerator. With my name on the container, he'd know they were from me.

The wine tasting was taking place in the barn. As I walked there, I thought about the momentary emotion I'd experienced. I'd been trying to deny it, but I think it was time for me to admit to myself I was on the verge of wanting to start a relationship with Scott that was more than just friendship.

My arrival at the meeting place allowed me to put off my thoughts until later…which was fine with me and had been the tack I'd taken with Scott since meeting him. A painful divorce had left me shying away from any romantic involvement.

The rows of chairs had been replaced by a long table covered with a white tablecloth. Rows of different-sized wineglasses practically filled the entire tabletop. I remembered the flight of merlots Phil had taken me on where I tasted the same type of wine from different years.

Five men and one woman chatted with each other in a familiar way, clearly comfortable with each other's company. Carlo and Lorenzo Sagatini were among them. Phil sat at a separate table making notes. He stood when he saw me and waved me over. We joined the group, and he introduced me. I asked them to call me Kelly, and they reciprocated with the same request of me to use their first names. All of them invited me to visit their wineries for a private tour, and I assured them I'd take them up on their offers.

"Okay, everyone, time to get started. I've arranged for a vertical flight as well as a horizontal flight. I've covered the labels so you can't bring any of your past knowledge to what you taste. The wines will be referred to by number."

The others nodded and sat at the table. I frowned. Vertical and horizontal?

Phil chuckled at my obvious bewilderment. "In a vertical tasting, you taste the same type of wine from one winery produced in different years. You can compare what the wine tastes like in different climate situations. In a horizontal flight, you choose one type of wine made in one year and sample that wine, say a merlot, from any number of different producers."

The tasting began, and I learned what Phil had meant by "enobabble." Words like blunt, briary, and supple swirled around me as the glasses clinked. I figured my best course of action was to sip, keep quiet, and listen. I would occasionally notice something I thought tasted like citrus or had a nutty flavor, but I wasn't about to believe I would ever excel at wine tasting.

Phil's brow furrowed as he tasted wine number five. "This doesn't taste right to me. What do the rest of you think?"

An older man I'd been introduced to as Angelo Cacciaroni took a sip. "Tastes fine to me, Phil."

Lorenzo Sagatini tasted his. "I agree with him. It has distinct oak flavor I find very pleasing to the palate." He glanced at Phil. "I hope you're not losing your ability to analyze wine."

Phil's frown deepened, then he shrugged his shoulders. "I have a bottle of this at home. It'll be interesting to compare them when I get back there next week." He swirled and sniffed the wine then shrugged again.

The tasting and the wine talk continued until all the bottles had been sampled.

Carlo Sagatini stood. "Phil, thank you for this opportunity to taste fine wine and enjoy lively conversation. We winemakers don't often have time to get together like this. There is always so much to do, no matter the season."

The others nodded and thanked Phil as well.

Lorenzo picked up his coat. "Sorry to hear about your friend Eric being killed."

Phil's mouth took a downward turn. "Yes. He's a big loss to the wine community. I know he was doing some work for you."

Lorenzo nodded as he slipped on his jacket. "Yes. I was worried that Eric's—you know his death and all—would delay the deal to sell the winery and jeopardize the real estate plans I have. The good news is the paperwork is far enough along that I think the sale will go through in a timely manner."

Phil didn't mention anything about Eric's death being murder, and I didn't feel it was my place to bring it up.

As I helped Phil put the glasses and wine bottles into boxes, I said, "It's so awful that Eric is gone."

He stopped for a moment. "I know. He was such a bright, promising young man. Hard worker. Always cheerful."

Phil put the last bottle away. He had been instructed to leave the boxes there and told the veterans would store them. We walked out together.

Phil's frown returned, and he shook his head. "Kelly, I'm worried. I wonder if I've lost my sense of taste. As I explained to you yesterday, everyone has a different sense of taste and smell. I can live with one person not noticing when a wine isn't right, but for both of them to feel that way…it must be me."

"Can that happen to a person?" I asked.

"Absolutely. Age can do it as well as allergies or respiratory infections and certain medicines. There are other causes as well. An infection can be cured, but if it's age, it could mean the end of my career."

"Phil, it's too early for you to start thinking that way. Like you said, a reduced sense of taste can happen for many reasons."

"You're right. I'll make a doctor's appointment when I get back to the inn."

Another thought crossed my mind. Was someone intentionally sabotaging Phil's sense of taste? Far-fetched, but having worked a number of cases with the Silver Sentinels, my mind had a tendency to turn to criminal actions.

"Phil, is it possible someone could be trying to destroy your ability to taste? You said drugs can alter what you taste. Has anyone given you any food or drink recently as presents?"

The shock in his voice matched the surprise on his face. "Kelly, what are you suggesting?"

"I'm not suggesting, I'm just considering possibilities. Do you have any rivals? Is there anyone who might be trying to get your job?"

Phil shook his head. "Not that I know of…but I'll think about it, as well as make a list of any gifts I've received."

"It's highly unlikely, but let's keep an open mind."

We reached our cars and went our separate ways. I went back into the community center to see if Scott was there. What I found in the kitchen instead was Cassie at the center island, tears rolling down her cheeks, and her eyes red and puffy.

I walked up to her and put my hand on her arm. "Cassie, what's the matter?"

She put the carrot down that she'd been grating and met my gaze. "I told Ian I wanted a trial separation, that his jealousy was out of control. He put his fist through the wall of our room. I took him to the hospital."

I gasped.

A temper combined with lack of control. Had he had another encounter with Eric? Had he killed Eric in a fit of rage?

Chapter 7

Cassie's voice quavered. "He has his own car here, but I didn't want him driving with what I figured was a broken hand. I still love the guy, but our situation needs to change." Her hands clenched. "When I go back to get him at the hospital, I'm going to ask him to leave. He wasn't planning to stay the whole time, so he might as well go now."

"I understand." I didn't want to make the situation more difficult for her, but I might not have another opportunity to ask. "Do you know if he got into any fights yesterday?"

Cassie patted her face with a tissue and blotted her eyes. "Not that I know of, but we weren't together the whole time." She frowned. "Why do you ask?"

She'd know sooner or later about Eric. "Eric, the man who helped you with the groceries, was killed last night."

She became still. "That's awful...but you aren't suggesting Ian had something to with his death, are you?"

"Cassie, I'm just asking. You yourself said his jealousy is out of control."

Cassie began shaking her head. "Ian gets angry, but kill someone? No."

She tried to sound definite, but a hint of doubt crept out with her denial.

"I have another meeting to attend." I gave her my card. "If there's anything I can help you with, please call me."

"Thanks." Cassie went back to grating her carrot with a somber look. I went out the back door, got in my Jeep, and followed the directions Gertie had given me.

I pulled into an empty gravel parking lot and got out. A white picket fence separated the garden from the parking area. The sign on the gate said, "Welcome to Esther Fallbrook's Garden." I went in and followed a winding path through a grove of tall redwoods.

The path turned to the right, and I found myself in an enchanted garden from a fairy tale. A profuse amount of red and yellow flowers lining the path bathed me in their sweet scent. Wooden chairs nestled amongst large feathery ferns and benches dotted the well-kept lawn. A chorus of birds sang a variety of songs unique to their species.

A bench with a scrimshaw design provided the perfect place for Sleeping Beauty to rest with tall stalks of lilies waving gently in the breeze on both ends. I expected to see Snow White dancing down the path followed by her minions. I wouldn't have been surprised if a sparkling white unicorn trotted past me.

Gertie had instructed me to keep going past the glen. The cottage was on the far side of the garden, out of sight. I came to another fence and this time the sign said "Private. No Admittance." I went through and around another corner and discovered a charming white bungalow. Giant trees towered over it and emphasized its diminutive size.

A massive array of flowers in many different hues had been planted around it. An artist had painted flowers matching the real ones on the side of the building and the colorful artwork continued the flowers up one side of the house and over the entryway.

I walked up a path of patterned stone tiles and knocked on the door.

The door opened, revealing Gertie. "Glad you could make it, Kelly. Come on in."

Rupert was standing behind her. I entered and found a comfortable-looking living room on my right with inviting over-stuffed chairs. A rocking chair with a needlepoint pillow occupied one corner. A compact dark green velvet couch rested against a wall. A glass-topped coffee table with a decorative white crocheted doily in the center was in front of it.

"This way," Rupert said.

I followed him to the kitchen and dining area and stopped. I shook my head as if to clear it. I'd just stepped into a crime scene show. Photos covered the walls showing men, white delivery-type vans, and motels interspersed with pictures of mounds of plants. Corkboards had been brought in to accommodate the number of photos and had been placed on the kitchen counters.

"Wow," was all I could muster in response.

Rupert's face bore a wide grin. "We've been busy."

"I'll say," I responded.

"These are the men we suspect of being poachers." Rupert pointed to labels under the photos. "These are the motels they are staying at in Fort Peter. The police can't do anything until there's concrete evidence, so we're trying to help with that."

Gertie joined in. "The Succulent Saviors carry cameras with them at all times in case they see something suspicious."

"I noticed the cameras this morning when they stopped us."

"Sorry about that," Rupert said. "We could tell you were picking plants, just not what kind."

"I understand."

Gertie went over to a folder on the counter. "Rupert made copies of the data the Succulent Saviors have gathered. I'll read it over tonight so I can report to the group tomorrow."

I took out my phone. "I'll take pictures of the information on the walls and boards. I can send them to the group and get copies of the photos made. We can start our own collection of pictures."

"Thank you for helping us, Rupert," Gertie said.

"My pleasure. I'm thrilled the Silver Sentinels are taking on the poachers."

Rupert's phone pinged, alerting him to a text. He read the message then let out a loud, "Yippee! The police have arrested three poachers and confiscated a truckload of plants."

"Great news!" Gertie said. "How long before we'll be able to have the plants so we can replant them?"

"I don't know, but the wardens have been getting them to us as fast as they can. I'll send out a message to everyone when I know."

Gertie turned to me. "The members of the garden club are dedicated to saving as many of the Dudleya farinosa as they can. They're delivered to Rupert's home because he has a potting shed the size of a small house."

Rupert nodded. "Once I send out a meeting time, as many of the members come to help as possible. We sort out the plants that are healthy enough to immediately go back into the ground on the cliffs. A group quickly leaves with them."

"The rest of us pot the remaining ones and categorize them as to their level of need," Gertie added.

I glanced at one board which had numerous photos of piles of plants. With their roots exposed, I knew they wouldn't live long.

I started taking pictures. "Where did they find the poachers?"

"Drake's Cove," Rupert replied.

Drake's Cove. That was where Eric went off the road…and maybe where he was murdered. I told Rupert and Gertie what I had learned about Eric's death and where he'd been found.

Rupert frowned. "I'll pass the news on to the members of the group. We don't know if the poachers had anything to do with the young man's demise, but I think it's a good idea for people to be even more cautious."

I finished taking my photos and then we all left, Rupert locking the building behind us.

"The grounds are lovely. Your club is doing a magnificent job," I said.

Gertie tapped along beside me with her cane. "We enjoy caring for it. Esther was such a dear to deed it to the community for all to enjoy."

Rupert joined in. "It can be reserved for weddings and parties and the like. Please let your guests know. Those events bring us upkeep money."

"I certainly will. I'll come back with my camera sometime soon and add the information and photos to our guest notebook."

"Thanks," Rupert said as we entered the parking lot.

My car was the only one in it.

"Would either of you like a ride?"

Gertie shook her head. "No, thanks, dear. I'm meeting a friend a couple of blocks from here. The walk will be good for me."

Rupert nodded. "My home is not too far from here. I like the exercise as well. Thanks for the offer."

The two of them walked off, and I drove back to the inn.

Helen was placing crackers on a tray and Julie was drying a large pot.

Tommy bounded in with Fred right behind him and tossed his backpack on the floor near the counter. "Hi, Mom!"

"Hi, honey. I made a snack for you." She removed plastic wrap from a small plate. "I baked granola bars today."

He sat on a stool and reached for the plate. "Yum. I love those."

Meanwhile, Fred approached Rex and went into play posture—front end down, back end up.

Julie smiled. "This would be a good time for Rex to be off duty. Do you have some place the dogs can play? Rex doesn't get a chance to do that very often."

"Sure. We have a fenced yard," Helen said. "Tommy, why don't you take your snack and the dogs over to our house?"

He slid off his stool. "Sure."

"Rex minds really well, so you don't need a leash."

Julie put the pot on the counter and went over to Rex, now sitting at attention.

"Rex, off duty," she said. The dog cocked its head to one side. "I know. You don't hear that command very often. Off duty. You're free to play."

Rex spun around and mirrored Fred's play pose.

"Wait, you two," Helen said to the dogs. "Outside."

Tommy grabbed the remaining granola bar. "Come on, Fred, Rex. Let's go play."

The three ran out the door, and I saw Tommy open the gate to their yard. The dogs raced through it and jumped, spun, and chased each other. Happy dogs!

I'd noticed Andy Brown's car when I drove in. "I'm going to say hi to Andy, then I'll be back to help with the evening appetizers."

Helen pulled a package from the refrigerator. "Okay. Andy brought us some new cheeses to try. I'll put some out for the guests."

Andy, a very knowledgeable cheesemonger, supplied cheese for the inn. He constantly surprised us with new choices from around the world.

I walked to the building housing Andy and Phil. It had a common area shared by the guests. I found them there absorbed in an assortment of wines and as well as cheeses in a wide array of sizes and colors. Both had binder paper they were filling with copious notes.

Andy and I exchanged hugs. The guys shared a little about what they were looking for in their wine and cheese pairings, and I expanded my ever-growing vocabulary related to the worlds of wine and cheese.

Phil was all smiles and excitement as they shared their ideas with each other. The two had been buddies for years. I was glad Andy was there what with Eric's death. Phil needed a good friend. I bid them adieu and returned to the main house.

The work area was empty. I checked the fire and the appetizers in the parlor. Everything looked good, so I went to my quarters and made a simple dinner of leftover baked chicken, steamed zucchini, and brown rice. I checked emails and then sent the photos I'd taken at the garden club to the Sentinels, along with an explanation. Returning to the parlor, I retrieved the evening guest dishes, cleaned them, and put the evening appetizers away.

As I went to bed, thoughts of Eric and Drake's Cove worked their way into my mind. Had Eric come upon some of the poachers? Had they killed him? Had the possible violence the warden mentioned begun?

Chapter 8

The next morning the doorbell interrupted our breakfast routine of retrieving baskets and cleaning up. Helen was washing dishes, and I'd just emptied the last basket.

"I'll get it," I said.

Glass panels on either side of the door revealed two police officers.

I opened the door. "Hello, Bill. What can I do for you?"

I didn't recognize the other officer. I wondered what had brought the two men here.

"Good morning, Ms. Jackson. Is Phil Xanthis here? We'd like to talk to him."

Ms. Jackson. Uh, oh. Apparently, Deputy Stanton and I are on formal terms once again.

When I first came to Redwood Cove, I helped the Silver Sentinels solve a murder. During the course of that investigation and a couple of others, Deputy Stanton and I never used first names. After I had been in town for a while and became the permanent manager of Redwood Cove Bed and Breakfast, we agreed to address each other on a first name basis, provided we weren't involved in a case together.

Official police business involving me in some way had started.

"I saw him a little while ago when I picked up the breakfast baskets. I believe his van is still in the parking lot…so he's probably here. I'll lead you to his room."

"Thanks. We appreciate it," Stanton said.

"This is Deputy Sheriff Davidson," Stanton said as he turned to the other officer. "Kelly Jackson is the manager of this inn."

I nodded at him and Davidson touched the brim of his hat. As I stepped outside to join them, the cold ocean breeze made me wish I'd grabbed a jacket. The sleeves of my blouse ended just below the elbow, and goose bumps covered my arms.

We climbed the stairs and stopped in front of Phil's room.

"This is it," I said.

Stanton knocked. He hadn't asked me to leave, so I decided to wait and see what was up.

Phil opened the door. He wore a white shirt, one of his embroidered wine vests, and black slacks.

He frowned. "Good morning, Deputy Stanton. What can I do for you?"

I hoped it wasn't more bad news, like he'd received regarding Eric.

"We have some questions for you. May we come in?"

"Certainly." He opened the door wide.

I turned to go.

"Ms. Jackson, I'd like you to stay," Deputy Stanton said. "I have some questions for you as well."

Not a good sign.

The room had a couch, a desk with a chair, and a queen-sized bed. Phil sat on the bed, I took the chair, and the officers sat on the couch. They both pulled out notepads.

Stanton flipped his open. "Where were you last night?"

"Here asleep. I went to bed around ten," Phil answered. "What is this about?"

Stanton turned to me. "Ms. Jackson, during the course of the night, did you have reason to look in the parking lot? And if so, did you see Mr. Xanthis's van?"

"No. It was a quiet night, and I went to bed around ten as well."

"Mr. Xanthis, may we see your van?" Stanton asked.

"Of course." Phil picked up keys from the desk, and we followed him to the parking lot. He stopped at his white delivery van.

Deputy Sheriff Davidson said, "Please open the back door."

Phil did as instructed and gasped when he saw what was inside. "Where did those cases come from? Those aren't mine."

Five white boxes had Eagle Ranch Winery written on the side of each one.

Deputy Sheriff Stanton answered, "Those were stolen last night from a high-end wine store."

Deputy Sheriff Davidson said, "Video cameras showed a van like yours at the scene and the license plate on that vehicle matches yours."

"I recognized your name when the information came in and knew you were staying here," Stanton said.

"The man in the video looks like you," Davidson added.

There was no pause between statements, and I felt the tension increase. I wondered if the rapid-fire pace and alternating between officers was a technique to make Phil say something he might be hiding.

"Would you like to change what you told us earlier about what you were doing last night?" Davidson asked.

Phil's face reddened "No. I have no idea where that wine came from or why the video shows a van like mine. What I told you was the truth."

Deputy Stanton moved in front of Phil. "Mr. Xanthis, I'm placing you under arrest for burglary and the possession of stolen property."

"I didn't steal anything!" Phil shouted.

The other officer had taken out handcuffs. "Put your hands behind your back."

Phil's hands were balled into fists. Deputy Sheriff Davidson grabbed one hand and pulled it behind Phil's back, put a cuff on it, then pulled his other arm back and cuffed it as well.

Phil looked at me, fear and despair showing on his face.

"Phil," I said. "I'll get in touch with Michael Corrigan. He'll know what to do."

"Kelly, tell him I'm innocent. I swear it's the truth."

"I will."

The officers led Phil to their patrol car. I watched as they helped him into the back seat.

I hurried to the inn and took a shortcut to the office through the parlor. I sat at the desk and dialed Corrigan's number. The sound of his hearty "Hello" made my tense shoulders drop a notch. I explained what had taken place.

"I'm on it, Kelly. I'll get an attorney and make bail. I've known Phil for years. He's part of our team. We'll get this sorted out."

"Thanks, Michael."

After we said goodbye, I sat at the desk thinking about what had just happened. I believed Phil when he said he hadn't stolen the wine, so that meant someone framed him. Who would do that and why? What could I do to help?

The Silver Sentinels.

They knew Phil and considered him a good friend. He helped on one of our recent cases. The group was meeting at noon, so I texted them about what had happened and asked for their help. Their answers were swift in coming. Of course they'd help Phil. I requested we meet an hour earlier, at eleven, if possible, and I would supply sandwiches for lunch. Again, their answers came quickly. They'd all be there.

I went to the work area and felt relieved Helen wasn't in the kitchen. I didn't want to explain what had happened. Going over it again would only bring Phil's distraught face to mind. I texted her the meeting had been moved to eleven. The clock said nine. The morning chefs would be here shortly to practice their recipes.

Back in my quarters, I checked emails. Once we got rolling on Phil's situation, I knew time would be in short commodity. A text from Michael said Phil would be out by late morning and back at the inn around noon. Michael had arranged for a rental car to be delivered to the police station for him. He hired private investigators to examine Phil's van when the police granted permission.

I grabbed a manila envelope from my file cabinet and went to the market, which was more of a general store. I ordered sandwiches and went to print the photos of the possible poachers I'd taken at the garden club's office. Another text from Michael alerted me that he'd arranged to get a copy of the video from the wine shop, and it would be delivered to the inn. I picked up lunch and with my envelope of pictures, headed back.

I went in the side door that allowed me to go to my quarters without going through the main workroom. I didn't feel like getting into a conversation at the moment. I put the sandwiches in the refrigerator and tossed my fleece on the couch. In the conference room, I posted the photos and put several sheets of chart paper on the walls. Different colored felt pens went on the table. Keeping busy kept Phil's situation at a distance. A half hour remained before the group would arrive, so I went to see if any new emails had come in.

The more I thought about the situation, the more I realized I needed to let Helen know what was happening—both with Phil's arrest and Eric's murder. I returned to the conference room and found her readying the place, as usual, with thermoses of coffee and hot water for tea as well as a pitcher of water.

"Helen, there have been some new developments. That's why the meeting was moved up. I want to share what's been taking place."

I filled her in on Phil's arrest and what Michael had already done. Then I took a deep breath. I didn't want to scare her, but Eric's murder and the possibility poachers were involved meant there was a potential danger to her and Tommy. I knew they occasionally walked on the headlands.

"There's more. Eric's death wasn't an accident."

I explained what the police had found and that poachers had been arrested where Eric's body had been discovered.

"At Monday's meeting, a ranger warned us to be careful when we were foraging."

Helen shook her head. "Thanks for telling me. I've seen some articles about the plant poaching but didn't think about the fact there might be danger."

"There's no evidence as yet the poachers are involved in what happened to Eric, but I wanted you to know."

"Tommy and I will be careful where we walk until this gets resolved."

"There's a very dedicated group of plant lovers called the Succulent Saviors who are working hard to catch the thieves. The Silver Sentinels will be helping them."

"I wish you luck and speed in finding answers for Phil as well as putting the poachers out of business." She glanced at the beverages. "If you run out of anything, let me know. I'm staying close by in case the chefs need help with anything."

"Shall do."

It was close to meeting time. I took out the dog bed for Princess and straightened the chairs. Voices in the hallway alerted me the group was arriving.

Mary walked in first with her usual load of purse, dog carrier, and container of sweets. I took the plastic box as she put her other items on the floor and let Princess loose.

Mary spied the dog bed. "Kelly, thank you for getting that out."

"You're welcome."

Princess made a beeline for it, curled up, and closed her eyes. The Chihuahua was usually a social butterfly, but obviously she was tired this morning.

"She's been playing with my sister's dog all morning," Mary said, by way of an explanation.

The others drifted in, got drinks, helped themselves to the muffins Mary had unveiled, and sat at the table.

Gertie banged the gavel on the table. "It's eleven. Let's get started."

I updated them with the news I had regarding Phil. "He should be here around noon. Michael is sending a copy of the video the police saw. I don't think there's much we can do until we have that and talk to Phil."

Nods of agreement accompanied my statement.

"Finding the poachers was to be our next project," the Professor said. "We didn't know at the time Eric was murdered."

Gertie nodded. "Our goal is safety for the community. I think we should try to find out who killed him."

"Terrible about Eric's death," Ivan said.

"His death has possibly taken a new turn with poachers being arrested near where his body was found," I said. "Finding the poachers and looking for Eric's killer go hand in hand."

Gertie gave a report on the Succulent Saviors' findings. The group was continuing to go out in teams and take photographs. Due to activity witnessed at the marina, they suspected the plants were being moved out on motor boats and probably taken to somewhere near San Francisco, where they were loaded into a container for transport. She handed out copies of the information the gardening group had put together, including a list of hotels and license plate numbers they believed were connected to the poachers.

She ended by saying, "As for the poachers, I don't see what we can add at this time to what Rupert and the Succulent Saviors are doing, other than keeping our eyes and ears open."

They scanned the photos.

Rudy sipped his tea. "They've done a thorough job."

The Professor put down his pen. "Since we've decided to investigate Eric's death, I feel we need to look into what he was involved in."

I chimed in. "I can help there. He was putting together an event for the hospital and helping with the sale of the Sagatini Winery."

Mary peeled the paper off of a muffin. "There's nothing that suggests danger in either of those activities, but we need to keep an open mind and do some research."

Gertie nodded. "I know people on the hospital event committee. I'll ask if Eric said anything to them about problems."

"I know several people on the volunteer staff. I'll see if some of them want to meet for breakfast," Mary said.

"Spots for events like that are a prize to obtain," Gertie said. "There's competition for who gets the booths. That being said, it's a small community and most of the vendors are on good terms."

The Professor pursed his lips. "I haven't been to Sagatini's in a while. I'll say I heard about the impending sale and wanted to get some of their wine in case the new owners didn't have the wine-making touch the family's known for. I'll see if the conversation leads anywhere helpful."

As the ideas had begun to come in, Rudy stood and recorded the comments on the charts. He labeled one "next steps," and wrote what people were going to do.

"Ivan and I can go to the marina and talk to our friends there and see for ourselves what's happening."

Helen entered with a package in her hand. "This just arrived. It's addressed to you and Michael."

She handed it to me.

"Thanks. It's the video." I stood. "I'll get my computer so we can watch it and grab the sandwiches too."

I returned with my laptop and lunch. As I set up my computer in a place where everyone could see the screen, the Professor and Mary unwrapped the sandwiches and put them on a platter he'd gotten out of the sideboard. Small plates and napkins were always kept out on the counter.

People filled their plates with a variety of sandwich quarters and refreshed their beverages. I was adjusting the computer screen when I heard a knock on the doorframe. I looked up and Phil stepped in. His pale face was haggard. Creases in his forehead and bags under his eyes made him look much older. His vacant stare spoke of a lost man.

I went over to him and gave him a quick hug. "We'll get this straightened out."

His shoulders sagged. "I've never been arrested. Being in jail, behind bars, is a frightening experience."

"I understand." I gave him another hug. "Why don't you get a cup of coffee? It might give you some energy for what's ahead. Help yourself to a sandwich. We have work to do to clear your name...which the Silver Sentinels and I will do."

At least I hope we will.

Phil smiled, and a glimmer of hope appeared in his eyes. "I know you've helped others in the past. You've solved a lot of cases."

He went to the counter and filled a mug with the dark, fragrant French roast Helen had put out, and dropped into one of the chairs at the table.

Mary rose and prepared him a plate with several sandwich pieces on it. As she placed it in front of him, she said, "You need to keep your strength up."

His weak smile seemed to confirm her words.

I opened the package and took out the video. "I think the first thing we need to do is look at the video that caused Phil to get arrested."

We all nodded in agreement, and I inserted it into the computer. The screen came alive, showing a man standing at an alarm box with his face shielded by a cap. I pushed the play button. The thief punched in numbers then opened an area on the side of the box and took out a key. He disappeared into the building.

The man, who appeared to be the same height as Phil, emerged and loaded a case into the back of a van. He repeated this four times, keeping his head down. The grainy picture made details hard to see. However, his curly hair resembled Phil's, and he wore a patterned vest similar to ones I'd seen Phil wear. The man put the key back, punched in the code, and left.

What little color had been in Phil's face when he entered the room drained away as he watched, leaving his Greek complexion the palest I'd ever seen it. As the scene ended, he sighed and ran his fingers through his short, tight curls. "That's my van, no doubt about it. I had custom equipment put in to secure the cases as I drove up the winding road to Redwood Cove. And the man in the video looks like me." He gazed around at the group. "I must have done it. I must have robbed the store."

Chapter 9

"Maybe I had a blackout of some kind." Phil shook his head and rested his head in his hands. "Either that, or I have a twin." He rubbed his face.

"We never saw the man's face," Rudy said. "There's no way to tell how much he looks like you."

I walked over to him and put my hand on his shoulder. "Phil, let's work on facts, not maybes."

The Professor stood and went to one of the pieces of chart paper. "Kelly's right. Let's start by listing what we know to be true, based on the video."

Mary went to the sideboard and started to fix herself another cup of tea. "I think we should examine closely what the person is wearing. Phil, you can tell us if he's got something on that you don't own."

Phil sat up a little straighter. "Good idea."

I started the video at the beginning.

"He knows the security code," Gertie said.

The Professor wrote that down.

Phil let out a low moan. "I know the code. They gave it to me when I was making a late delivery, as well as telling me the whereabouts of the key. I've known them for years, and they trust me...at least they used to."

"Let's start at the top of his head and look at his clothes," I said.

The man was wearing a baseball cap that said, "Welcome to Mendocino County Wine Country."

The image was in black and white, so we didn't know what color it was.

"Do you have a hat like that?" Mary asked.

"Yes. They're a dime a dozen and easy to come by," Phil replied.

I agreed with him. I'd seen the hat in many different colors for sale at numerous spots. The man's curly hair came up around the edges of the cap like Phil's. None of us pointed out the similarity. Next came the vest.

Phil frowned and leaned toward the screen. "I have several wine-patterned vests. Because of the poor quality of the picture, it's hard to tell what the decoration is. I don't believe I have one like that."

The light-colored shirt and dark pants were next. There wasn't enough detail for Phil to be able to say yea or nay to ownership. Next were the tasseled shoes the thief was wearing.

"I definitely don't have shoes like that," Phil said.

"Phil," I said, "you don't own those shoes, so you didn't do it."

In response, he gave me a weary, sheepish grin. "Thanks, Kelly. When I saw my van there, I thought maybe I was losing it."

"While the shoes are enough for you to be certain of your sanity, it's highly unlikely it will convince the police," the Professor said. "Let's keep working on the list. What other facts can we ascertain from what we saw?"

Phil nodded. "The man knows his wines. The most expensive and easy-to-sell ones were stolen."

The Professor wrote down Phil's comments and noted his van on the fact list. "Phil, how do you think your van got there?"

"I don't have any idea. It's old, so it doesn't have any of the fancy electronics of new vehicles. I imagine the old-fashioned way of hot wiring it."

"Have you loaned it to anyone?" I asked.

"No. No one's asked. It's my workhorse, and I use it pretty much on a daily basis."

Mary sat at her place with her hot tea. The sweet scent of peppermint greeted me.

"Any valet parking?" she asked.

That brought a laugh from Phil. A pleasant change from the despondent look he'd come in with. "No valet parking for me, Mary."

The Professor started another chart. "Questions. Who did it? Why frame Phil?"

Mary chimed in. "Who has the code besides Phil?"

I had kept my phone on in case Michael wanted to reach me. A text alert came in, and I read a message from him. Not good news.

The group stared at me expectantly.

"Michael's attorney just learned the only fingerprints the police found in the van were Phil's."

We all turned to look at the video. I leaned in to get as close a look as I could. There was no evidence of gloves on the thief.

Phil's face began to crumble.

"Phil," I said, "we'll figure out how that was done. Remember the shoes."

He rose. "I'm going to go to my room and make sure I don't have a pair like that. I don't trust my memory right now. Thank you, everyone, for your help and support."

Phil went out with a weary walk.

"We don't have a lot to go on, but we've been in that situation before," the Professor said. "Let's spend the afternoon learning as much as we can. If anything significant comes to light, get it out to the others."

"Will tomorrow at noon work for another meeting?"

They all said it would, and Gertie banged her gavel.

People gathered up their things, and I took the empty platter and plates to the kitchen. Helen would take care of the rest of the dishes and drinks. Handling the meeting space was one of her responsibilities.

I entered the kitchen area, put the dishes in the sink, and saw Sebastian leaning against the divider, checking his cell phone. There was no sign of Julie.

His head jerked up as I entered. "Hi, Kelly. Do you know where Julie is?"

"No. I figured she'd be here with you, cooking."

"She's supposed to be. We planned on beginning at one like we did yesterday. It's almost one thirty now."

"Maybe she had car trouble. I'll call the center and talk to Cassie. They were planning to forage together again today."

I called and Scott answered, "Hi, Kelly."

Caller ID was useful, but I was still caught off guard at times when someone knew who I was. "Hi. Sebastian and I are here waiting for Julie. Could I talk to Cassie? Maybe she knows where she is."

"If Cassie was here, you could, but she's not. We were supposed to meet at one. I just went over to the barn, and neither of them showed up for lunch. I heard Cassie asking some of the veterans where would be a good place to forage. I checked with them and they gave me the location she was going to try. I informed Michael, and he and Garl headed up there."

I began to feel the stirrings of apprehension. Enough time had passed that the women could have walked back to the center if they'd had automobile problems. The property wasn't that big.

"Garl's pickup just pulled in out front. I'll call you back."

I updated Sebastian on what I had learned…but didn't say anything about the fears I had. I noticed an oval metal device on the counter. It had holes in a number of different sizes and an open area that looked like the mouth of a fish.

"What's that?" I asked.

Sebastian picked it up, put his index finger through one of the holes, and began to twirl it. "It's a gift I bought for Julie as a thank you. It's a kale and herb razor. She went out of her way to teach me some cooking techniques yesterday. She told me chefs were always on the lookout for something that might help them save time."

"I'm sure she'll appreciate it."

Then there was silence as we waited for Scott's call. We didn't attempt any small talk. Both of us were worried.

My phone rang. "What's happening, Scott?"

"Michael found Julie's car with Rex in it. Neither of the women was there."

"Julie would never leave Rex alone willingly."

"I know."

Then I heard it.

The ringing of the fire station bell.

The call for search and rescue volunteers.

Chapter 10

When the bell started to ring, Sebastian pulled his apron off, threw it on the counter, and ran out the door.

"The police just drove in," Scott said. "Michael called them as soon as he got here then asked me to get the background I had on Julie."

"She gave me a detailed list of her contacts, as well as some other pertinent information in case something happened to her," I said. "I want to come out to the center to see if there's anything I can do to help. I'll bring her paperwork with me."

"Great," Scott said.

"The search and rescue bell is ringing," I said, "so it sounds like they've decided to put together search teams."

"I need to go talk to the officers and give them directions to where the vehicle was found," Scott said. "Michael and Garl went back to the area to search for Julie."

"Got it. I'll be there shortly."

I ended the call and rushed to the safe, where I'd put Julie's papers. I pulled the folder out and went to the copy machine. It was hard to take the time to make the copies because I was anxious to get to the center, but I willed myself to do it so I'd have backup pages.

Underneath the personal data Julie had given me was the form making me Rex's guardian. I hesitated. I didn't know how long it would be before we found Julie, and I might be bringing the dog back with me. I copied that as well then slipped all the papers into a manila envelope and put the originals back in the safe.

I paused as I thought about what might be ahead. There could be a lot of walking through brush and on muddy trails due to the rain we'd had a few days ago. I hurried to my room and switched my lightweight jeans for heavy denim ones and changed my leather walking shoes and lightweight socks for my hiking boots, along with thick wool socks. I put what I needed from my purse in my fleece's pockets and grabbed my down jacket.

As I drove to the center, I found myself in a stream of cars entering the area. I pulled into the parking area in front of the main building. Men and women were hurrying toward the barn. They wore sturdy black boots, thick leather belts, and vests with search and rescue written on them.

Search and rescue.

They were going to search for Julie.

My heart beat faster.

Most of the people had backpacks slung over their shoulders. I recalled when one of my brothers was part of a search and rescue team back home and he had prepared a "go" bag. I suspected the people here were carrying a change of clothes, water, leather gloves, and rope, among other things. Items they might need on an extended search or when they found someone.

A tent had been erected in front of the barn. An officer stood behind a table with a growing line of people in front of him. I guessed they were checking in.

It was organized chaos.

I stopped in front of the center's main building, and Scott came running out. His light tan boots shouted new. There wasn't a speck of dirt showing.

He opened my passenger door. "The police aren't letting people into the area where the car is parked. However, they asked for any background I had on Julie, so they'll let me through."

"I have information as well, including a document from Julie making me Rex's guardian if something happened to her."

Though Julie was thinking seizure, not going missing.

"Good. We should be allowed to pass then."

I drove toward the road Scott directed me to, passing the barn and driving slowly through the ever-growing crowd. I spotted Ian among the group, one hand in a cast. He hadn't gone home. Had Cassie changed her mind? Or had he decided to stay and keep track of her?

I stopped to let the community center's van go across the road in front of me. One of the veterans was driving it.

Scott waved at him and the man nodded back. "I told the police they could use the van to transport teams to their designated search areas as soon as they were assembled and ready to go."

The driver had stopped the van and rescuers were filing into it. A man with a clipboard checked them off as they climbed aboard.

"It's impressive how quickly they got organized," Scott said. "They already have an outline of the property on a bulletin board with search areas marked off. The veterans know the property very well and helped them by describing the terrain so they could better assemble their teams to deal with the conditions. The police want to cover as much territory as possible as quickly as they can. The tougher areas to navigate are smaller in size."

I reached the checkpoint the police had set up. We explained to the deputy our purpose and what we had with us, and he waved us on. It was a bumpy dirt road, but it didn't take us long to get to Julie's Subaru, where it was parked under a stand of redwood trees. I could see the outline of Rex's head in the back.

There were a number of officers milling around, using walkie-talkies. Pairs of deputies were walking what looked like a pattern that went farther and farther beyond the vehicle. Garl and Toby, his dog, stood off to the side. I parked under a mature redwood tree and Scott and I got out as Deputy Stanton approached.

Scott held up the papers he'd brought with him. "I have the information you requested."

"Thanks," Stanton said as Scott handed him the paperwork. Stanton scanned it. "I see a photo here. Can you text that to me? And Deputy Sheriff Davidson as well. I don't have cell phone service here, so I won't get it for a while."

"I can when I get back to my office."

"Good," Stanton gave him Davidson's number. "Do you know if Julie was foraging with anyone?"

"She had planned to partner with Cassie MacGregor," Scott said.

Stanton wrote in his notepad. "Do you know for certain that took place?"

"No," Scott replied. "But someone at the center might've seen them. I'll ask when I go back there."

"If they had foraged together, would they have driven separately or both taken Julie's vehicle?"

"Again, I don't know, but I'll work on finding out."

I took the envelope out from behind my driver's seat. "I have some additional information on Julie that she gave me in case something happened to her. I also have a form making me guardian of her dog, Rex. Julie has a history of seizures, though she hasn't had one for months, and wanted him to be taken care of in case of an emergency."

Stanton nodded. "I'm glad to hear that. I didn't like the thought of him going to the pound."

"Is it okay if I get him now? We don't know how long he's been in there."

"Sure, but I want to show you something first to see if you recognize it."

He went over to one of the police cars, put on latex gloves, took something out, and returned to where we were.

Stanton held up a blue cloth pouch with the design of a running dog on the side. "Have you seen this before?"

"That looks like the dog treat bag Julie showed me. If I can see what's inside, I might be able to tell you for sure."

He opened the bag. Inside were heart-shaped cookies with an R in the middle. "That's Julie's. She made the mold herself and bakes all of Rex's treats."

"Thanks for confirming it belongs to her. We found it near her car. I'll go with you to get Rex."

"I'll go get a leash in case his isn't there," I said.

I opened the back of the Jeep and pulled a duffel bag toward me. I had my own rescue bag of sorts. Years ago, I had vowed I would always stop to help a loose animal that was in danger, even if it meant missing an important appointment or an airplane flight. This was after watching car after car whiz by a shaking dog stranded on an island of a busy street, no one stopping to help. He came home with me and became mine when the owners couldn't be found.

The promise had led me into some interesting and sometimes challenging situations, but it was one I'd never regretted. I felt I'd saved a few animals along the way.

I opened the bag and took out a beach towel. You could throw it over the head of a growling dog to keep from getting bitten or blindfold a frightened horse to calm it down. Leashes, ropes, collars, collapsible bowls, dry dog food, and treats filled the bag. I grabbed a leash and went back to Stanton.

"We haven't had time to check for fingerprints yet," Stanton said as we approached the Subaru. "Don't touch anything."

He slowly opened the hatch.

As he did so, I said, "Stay, Rex. Stay," and put my hand up to grab his collar.

Stanton raised the back lid the rest of the way, and I snapped my leash onto the metal circle on his collar. Rex whined and stared at me as if imploring me to take him to his master. I only wished I could.

I pulled on his lead. "Come, Rex."

He willingly obliged.

Scott looked inside. "I see his leash." He looked at Stanton. "Is it okay if I take it?"

"I doubt if there's anything we'll get off of a cloth lead that would be helpful, but since Kelly has one, let's leave it for now. Whoever put him in the car most likely handled it."

"What about the bed? And I see a water bowl."

Stanton paused. "It's best to leave everything as it is. We don't know what's happened here yet. If a crime has been committed, there might be evidence there. We've seen nothing to suggest a struggle, but I don't want to take any chances."

I walked Rex away from Julie's vehicle and stayed out of the way of the police. My stomach tightened. Stanton had used the words "crime" and "struggle." I hoped Julie was okay.

Scott walked over to my vehicle and spread the towel out in the back.

Rex sniffed around and took care of business. After a few minutes, we walked back to Scott.

"Thanks for putting out the towel for Rex."

"You're welcome."

I patted the floor of the vehicle. "Rex, in."

He obeyed but didn't lie down. He kept staring out a side window, searching for his owner. A wire partition kept him in the back.

I took out the collapsible bowl from my bag, opened it, and started to walk to the other side of the car, where I kept containers of water in a side compartment.

Scott beat me to it. "Let me help."

He filled the bowl as I unsnapped the leash and gave Rex some pats on his head. I took off his service vest and paused, thinking of Julie. I looked forward to when he'd be wearing it again. I put it on the floor next to him and closed the hatch. I opened the windows a bit to allow the cool air into the vehicle. Garl and Toby were standing on the fringe of the action, and Scott and I joined them.

"Where's Michael?" Scott asked.

"That's what I'd like to know," Garl replied. "We were supposed to meet half an hour ago."

Garl went on to tell us he and Michael found two different paths Julie could have taken from where her car was parked. They'd decided to split up. The two of them knew about the warning regarding the poachers, but neither of them was concerned about their own safety. They had agreed on a time to meet.

But Michael hadn't shown up.

After taking the papers from us, Stanton and the other officers ignored us. I figured they didn't want us walking around, but we hadn't been told not to. "Garl, please take us to where you last saw Michael."

"You bet."

"Kelly," Scott said, "do you think Rex could help us find Julie?"

I thought for a moment then shook my head. "Highly unlikely. There's a lot of training involved in teaching a dog to track. There's more of a chance he'd accidentally destroy evidence, and we definitely don't want that to happen. We're already walking on thin ground as it is to stay here and search."

"Toby might do the same thing," Garl said. "I'll put him in the truck."

We circled around through the trees, keeping our distance from the police. We weren't hiding… just being quiet and discreet. We emerged a short distance from the split in the road, where Garl and Michael had parted.

Garl pointed. "I went this way, and he went that way."

We went Michael's way.

"Michael," Scott yelled.

No answer.

The trees gave way to rocky cliffs as we neared the ocean. The breeze picked up, and I was glad I had on my jacket. The wind brought a hint of fog with it. I zipped up and slipped my hands in my pockets. Rocks, nearby ocean… the description of the home of the sought-after succulent. The living "gold" that beckoned to the poachers.

The dirt road was mostly dry, except for muddy dips here and there where we could see footprints…a lot of them for a back road on private property.

Scott paused at one muddy patch. "There's been a lot of activity here, and I think I know why. This road continues to where it meets the highway a few miles ahead. We keep a locked gate across the entry, but it would be easy for someone to break in. The area is isolated, so it is unlikely poachers would be seen. I'll let the police know when we get back."

I frowned. "I don't see any paw prints, which makes me think Julie and Rex didn't come this way. He was trained to stay by her side, and I think she'd walk on the road for some of the time. She might leave it for a short while to forage, but when we harvested together, we only went a few steps off the path to pick a plant."

"It's possible she was…taken near her car," Scott said. "That area was grassy and prints wouldn't show…and that's where the treat bag was found."

I realized we hadn't said anything about kidnapping. It had gone unstated. But I knew Julie wouldn't leave Rex willingly. Again, the thought surfaced that someone had forced her to leave him.

She must've been abducted. Had she run into the poachers and they'd taken her?

The three of us walked along the side of the road so as to not destroy any tracks, carefully scanning the ground. I understood why Garl and Michael hadn't been concerned about the poachers. Both were a good size and fit, and anyone would think twice about attacking Garl with the Great Dane by his side.

Scott stopped, knelt down, and picked up a crumpled piece of paper. He unfolded it. "It's a ticket to an event Michael attended several nights ago."

So he came this way...but where is he now?

Garl pointed to an area with tire tracks. "This is the first sign of a vehicle."

There were good imprints showing the pattern of the tread, but there wasn't anything that seemed to distinguish them in any way. Maybe the police could find something.

Scott walked ahead a few feet to a dry, rocky spot in the road. "Let's cross to the other side. There are no prints to disturb here."

We followed him and went back to the muddy area. There were several footprints of average size belonging to at least two people...and two huge boot prints. The impressions were deep, and a large star imprinted the sole.

One right foot, one left.

They weren't going down the road, but toward the side of the tire tracks, as if someone was going to enter the vehicle. Smaller prints were on either side of the larger ones.

"The big ones are Michael's," Scott said.

"How can you be so sure?" I asked.

He lifted his foot and its now mud-spattered boot, turning it so Garl and I could see the bottom. "They're custom boots he gets from Texas. He talked me into getting a pair."

The bottom was identical to the imprint in the mud.

Scott put his foot back down. "I think it's safe to say there's a good chance Michael has been kidnapped."

Chapter 11

"There's no sign of a struggle," Garl said.

He was right. If there'd been a struggle, I would've expected to see areas where boots had slipped, prints overlapping each other, and gouges in the mud.

Instead, there were just clear footprints in a perpendicular path to the tire marks.

"I agree," Scott said. "They must have had a weapon or some kind of leverage to make him cooperate. I need to get back to the center. I'm guessing there will be a ransom demand made. Michael's wealth is well known."

Ransom. I shivered—and not just from the cold.

We walked back at a fast pace. Stanton and a new crew of officers with equipment boxes stood next to Julie's car. When the deputy saw us, he scowled in our direction.

"Wait! Let me explain," I said as I saw him open his mouth, getting ready to say something.

I didn't have to.

Scott stepped forward. "I have reason to believe Michael Corrigan might have been kidnapped."

"Why?" Stanton wasn't one to mince words.

Scott shared what we'd found and what he thought was going to happen. "I need to get back to the community center and be available for any attempts at contact the kidnappers might make."

"We need to see the area you're talking about," Stanton said.

Garl said, "I can take you there."

Scott handed Stanton the ticket he'd picked up. "This is the ticket I told you about. You know where I'll be if you need to reach me. If anything develops, I'll let Deputy Sheriff Davidson know so he can get in touch with you."

Garl and the officers left as Scott and I got in my vehicle. Rex greeted us with an anxious whine.

As I drove down the road, I glanced over at Scott. His mouth was set in a grim line, his jaw clenched.

"Scott, if anyone can take care of himself, it's Michael."

"I know…but a bullet can take down the strongest of men."

He was right.

I persisted. "But why would someone want to kill him? I can't imagine this is the time and place for an old enemy to be lying in wait for him. It's most likely the poachers. They have nothing to gain by killing him."

Scott nodded and appeared to relax a bit. "You're right. I hope if they're the ones responsible, they see it that way. If they want money, they'll have to prove to me he's alive."

As we approached the barn, I said, "I'll work on finding out whether or not Cassie went with Julie."

"Good. I'll call Michael's attorney and tell him what's happened. He'll be the one responsible for getting any money needed."

I parked in front of the center's building under a redwood tree, and Scott got out and trotted to the front door. His worry was palpable.

I got Rex out of the back and headed for the barn, hoping to find Sebastian. He'd be able to talk to the other veterans and find out what they knew about Cassie. I didn't have to look for Sebastian. He found me. I stepped into the building and Sebastian suddenly showed up at my side.

The corners of his mouth were turned down. "You have Rex. That must mean you haven't found Julie."

I could see he so desperately wanted some good news. I wracked my brain for any positive words or sign of hope I could give him. "Deputy Sheriff Stanton told us they hadn't found any sign of a struggle…maybe she and Cassie needed to do something without Rex."

From the look on his face, there was no comfort in those words.

"Please let me know as soon as you hear anything," Sebastian said.

"I will. What's your cell phone number?"

He told me and I put it in my phone, then gave him mine.

"Speaking of Cassie, I need your help. She and Julie planned to forage together this morning, but we don't know if they did or not. If they did leave together, the police want to know if she drove her own car. Can you talk to anyone who was here this morning and see if they know the answers to those questions?"

"Sure. Anything to help." The last words were said over his shoulder as he hurried out.

I went over and studied the board that had been erected to hold the map. Lines had been drawn in a grid format and each section given a number. The word "vehicle" identified the area where Julie's car had been found.

Deputy Sheriff Davidson approached. "May I help you?"

"I was just studying the map. Your organization and the speed with which you've gone into action is impressive."

"When a life is at stake, we do everything we can to move as quickly as possible."

I paused and then pointed to where I'd just been on the map. "I was up there helping to search. This is the dog left in the car."

"I heard about him." Just then his radio signaled and he stepped away from me. After a brief conversation, he returned, a serious look on his face. "It seems another person has gone missing. A man named Michael Corrigan...and it's being considered a possible kidnapping."

Davidson wrote the name on a chalkboard under the other name on it—Julie Simmons.

I nodded. "I was part of the group that found the evidence."

I briefly filled him in. I figured he would be provided more detailed information soon.

He left and Rex and I started back for the car. I wasn't sure what the Silver Sentinels and I could do to help, but we often came up with a plan when we put our heads together. I stepped off the sidewalk to let others pass and stood next to a van with Sagatini Winery in red letters on the side. I texted the group the latest news and asked if they could meet at four.

As I put the phone back in my jacket, I became aware of raised voices belonging to Lorenzo and his father, Carlo.

"I don't want to sell the winery," Carlo said. "I was hoping with Eric dead the deal would fall through."

Phil had been right about the father being upset.

"Dad, we've been through this a hundred times. You want to retire, and I don't want to run the winery. It's as simple as that. You'll still have your home and twenty acres...and time to enjoy your life."

"Lorenzo, you can hire a winemaker. You can hire a manager. They can run the business and the family name and our heritage can continue on. You're a fourth generation Sagatini. It's more than a winery. It's our name, our family's business."

"No." The answer was firm. "Trust me. The best plan is to sell."

I hadn't intended to eavesdrop, but the truth was, I was listening to someone's private conversation, and an angry one at that. It was time to make myself known. I stepped onto the path and walked past the van to the back of it. Lorenzo and Carlo had exchanged their tailored Italian suits for khakis and denim shirts.

Just as I became visible, Lorenzo tossed a case of water onto a hand truck with such force his father, who was holding the equipment upright, had to step back.

He saw me then turned to his father. "Sorry, Dad. I didn't mean to throw it so hard."

"No harm," his father said. "Kelly, good to see you again, though I wish it was under better circumstances."

No sign of the anger I'd heard showed in either of their faces. Even with the bitter differences, they'd come together as family. Their issues would stay in-house. They'd closed ranks.

Lorenzo placed another case on the dolly, more gently this time. "We got news of the search and rescue effort and the teams assembling. Dad and I supply water and help with the food if that becomes necessary."

I saw large containers of water in the back of the vehicle.

Lorenzo followed my gaze. "We ask people to refill their water bottles to keep down the number of plastic containers used."

Carlo turned the hand truck in the direction of the barn. "I'll take these over."

"Okay," Lorenzo said. "I'll get the rest of the water out."

He turned to me. "Bad news about Phil getting arrested for stealing wine. Hard to believe he'd do something like that. People can surprise you."

A flash of anger surged through me. What happened to innocent until proven guilty?

"Then don't believe it, because he didn't do it." My words were clipped and overly loud.

Lorenzo's eyes widened and his eyebrows rose. His shocked expression reflected the harshness in my voice.

"Sorry. I apologize for talking to you like that. I'm on edge with all that's happened."

"I understand. I like Phil, and I'm glad you believe in him."

"The Silver Sentinels and I are working to prove him innocent of the theft."

"I'm happy to hear he has you and the others helping him out. This must be a very difficult time for him, with Eric's death and then his ability to taste in question, which could mean the end of his career."

"Yes."

There wasn't much more I could say. It was a very hard time for Phil.

Lorenzo's father returned and I continued with Rex to my Jeep. I checked my phone for messages. The Sentinels would be at the inn at four. I was about to put the dog in the back when I saw Sebastian in the distance walking toward the barn.

"Rex, let's go see what Sebastian found out."

I found him questioning Jim Patterson, the farm manager. I stood next to them as Sebastian asked him about Cassie.

"I didn't see her this morning," Jim said. "Sorry I can't be more helpful."

Sebastian thanked Jim and turned to me. "I still have a few more people I can talk with, but two of them have said they saw Cassie follow Julie's Subaru in her Volkswagen."

I shook my head. "That means she's missing as well as her car."

The list of missing people continues to grow.

"Could the two of them have gotten away in her Beetle?" he asked.

It was a futile hope and he knew it. I could tell by the desperate look on his face.

"If they did, why haven't they contacted us? And why leave Rex?" I asked.

"Right." The word had a hopeless ring to it.

"I need to get the news to Stanton about Cassie," I said.

I saw Deputy Sheriff Davidson, went to him, and told him what we'd learned.

He picked up his radio from the table where it rested. "Thanks. I'll let the others know."

"I have photos of Cassie's car. It's very distinctive. Stanton doesn't have cell reception where he is. I can text them to you so you can distribute them."

"I appreciate that. As I said, we want to act as quickly as possible in a situation like this. The manager here, Scott Thompson, sent me a photo of Julie Simmons. I'll check with him and see if he has one of this young woman."

"He should. The chefs provided photos for a brochure he created."

Davidson gave me his number. The photos were on my phone, and I was able to send them to him within a matter of minutes. I glanced at the chalkboard. A third name had been added—Cassie MacGregor.

I rejoined Sebastian. "There's something else you should know. It's been made public now. Michael Corrigan is missing, and it's believed he's been kidnapped."

Michael made it a habit to know all the veterans personally, so, while I hadn't seen Sebastian with him, I knew he'd know who he was.

"Now Michael and Cassie both gone." He shook his head. "Along with—"

Out of the corner of my eye, I saw Ian approaching. He stopped in front of Sebastian, his uncast hand clenched. "Did I hear you say my wife Cassie has disappeared with a man named Michael?"

Anger contorted his face and the demons of jealousy stared out from his eyes. Again, I wondered if he had had another encounter with Eric. And with his uncontrollable temper, was it possible he had something to do with Cassie, Michael, and even Julie disappearing?

Rex leaned into my leg.

Startled, Sebastian stepped back. "No...no...they've both gone missing. The police are thinking kidnapping."

Ian shook his head in disbelief. "My Cassie is a fighter. She wouldn't let someone take her. She's run off with him, that's what's happened."

I'd had enough. My temper was on the short side today, and I stepped toward the big man. "Ian, we haven't been introduced, but I know who you are."

He turned to me. "I remember you helping Cassie when she spilled the groceries."

"Right. First, you didn't let Sebastian finish. Julie is missing as well and her service dog was left behind. The police believe Michael's been abducted, so there's a good chance that's what has happened to Cassie and Julie."

The anger began to dissipate and was replaced by a puzzled frown. "Kidnapped? Why would someone kidnap Cassie? We have no money to speak of. Does someone want to hurt her?"

"We don't know anything yet," I said.

His free hand formed a fist. "No, that can't be...that someone took her by force. Cassie's always been able to take care of herself. She's got to be okay."

"Second, you referred to her as your Cassie. Based on a recent conversation I had with her, at the rate you're going, she may not be your Cassie much longer."

Sebastian moved away out of earshot to give us privacy.

Ian's lips tightened. "Is she seeing someone else?"

"Not that I know of. She and I had a talk after you broke your hand. I know how it happened and why and that she wanted you to leave." I pointed to his cast. "It's your temper and your jealously that's the problem."

Ian sat abruptly in a nearby chair, rubbed his face, then ran his fingers through his hair. "I love her so much. I'm away from home a lot. I'm a long-distance driver and spend long hours driving dark roads. My mind winds down twisty paths and creates unpleasant scenarios. I know I'm driving her crazy, but the last thing I want to do is lose her. I don't know what to do."

I sat next to him. "She loves you."

"She told you that?"

I nodded. "Yes, so your relationship isn't over yet."

How has this turned into a counseling session? And with me, of all people, still recovering from my divorce giving advice?

"Have you seen a marriage counselor?"

"Yes, when we can. Our schedules are so different. It's difficult to find a time that works for both of us." Worry clouded his voice. "Do the cops really think they've been kidnapped?"

I nodded. "When they find her, you'll have your chance to mend your marriage."

I definitely didn't want to use the word "if."

"By the way, my name is Kelly Jackson, manager of the Redwood Cove Bed and Breakfast."

"Nice to meet you," Ian said.

I stood and Sebastian came back over to us.

He stopped in front of Ian. "My name is Sebastian Reynolds. Julie and I worked together yesterday. I really like her. Her disappearance has been very hard to take. I can't imagine what it must be like for you with your wife missing."

Ian looked at him with distraught eyes.

"Listen," Sebastian said, "those of us who live here are beginning to put together food for the searchers. I think keeping busy is the best thing we can do right now. We're not members of search and rescue, so we can't join the teams. Why don't you come and help us?"

Ian stood, a slow, heavy movement, as if the world was on his shoulders. In a way, it was…the world of worry for his Cassie.

"Thanks. That's a good idea. My name's Ian MacGregor."

The two shook hands then walked away in the direction of the main building. I followed a distance behind, lost in my own thoughts. The stark reality of the situation had settled in. Three people missing. I hoped they were together and could support one another. If it was the poachers who had taken them, hopefully they just wanted them out of the way to continue their stealing. But then, why not just get rid of them? I shook my head. I needed to stop going down my own dark path.

I took Rex with me into the main building, wanting to see if Scott had learned anything. He'd created a private office for himself in one of the rooms off the lounge. The door was closed, and I knocked.

"Come in." Scott was staring at a notepad but turned and looked at me as I opened the door.

"Is there any news?" I asked.

"Yes. I got a call, a ransom demand." He tossed the pen he'd been holding onto the desk. "It's official. Michael's been kidnapped."

Chapter 12

"What!" I exclaimed.

"They want a million dollars by tomorrow and said they'd call in the morning with instructions. Michael's attorney is getting it together. It'll arrive tomorrow by way of an armored truck. I've told the police." Scott leaned back. "Now there's nothing for me to do but wait."

"Did they say anything about Julie and Cassie?"

"No." Scott put his elbows on his legs and dropped his head into his hands. "Michael's a good man. He doesn't deserve anything bad to happen to him."

I pulled a chair next to his, sat, and put my hand on his arm. Rex settled at my feet. "It'll all work out. The ransom means he's probably still alive."

"I believe he is. I told them they'd have to show a photo of him holding the *San Francisco Chronicle* with the date on it. They agreed to that."

Smart thinking on Scott's part. Our local paper came out only once a week and that was yesterday.

"I'm convinced he saved my mother's life. I'd do anything for him."

With only waiting ahead, I felt talking would be good medicine to fill the time. "How did he do that?"

"She and Dad were on vacation in China in a remote area of the country. Not the type of trip they usually took, but they decided to try something different. She became gravely ill. The kind of medical care she needed wasn't available."

He went on to tell me as he began to frantically make plans for getting her help, Michael learned of the situation.

Scott's voice, husky with emotion, continued, "He came to me and said his private jet was being readied, along with a medical team. They'd be flying out within the hour."

I squeezed his arm. Scott put his hand over mine.

"He contacted associates in Beijing and said medical specialists would go to the village by helicopter and bring Mom and Dad back to the best hospital in the city...and that's what happened. Mom is alive and well today, thanks to him. Like I said, I'd do anything for the man."

He rose, went to his desk, and took a sip from a coffee cup. I was sure it must have been cold by now. I checked my watch. I still had a little time before I needed to leave to meet the Silver Sentinels.

"How did you meet Michael?"

He sat again. "I was working for a resort when a tornado struck and ripped it apart. Michael owned a property nearby that wasn't damaged. He took in all of our guests and only charged the owners whose property was destroyed operating costs."

I nodded. "All I've ever heard are good things about him."

Scott continued, "That's Michael. The company that owned the destroyed property decided not to rebuild. Michael offered me a job and here I am today."

It was time for me to go. A thought struck me. "Scott, the Silver Sentinels and I planned to meet today at four to brainstorm what we can do to help find Julie, Cassie, and Michael. Why don't you join us?"

Scott gazed at me quizzically. "What can they do? There are hundreds of people searching, police have been notified...I don't see anything left but to wait."

"They're amazing when they combine their knowledge, and they have a lot of contacts from living here so long. They've never failed to come up with a plan yet."

He shook his head. "Maybe the kidnappers will call again...and want something else."

"Leave one of the veterans in charge of the phone. That person can call you with any messages."

Scott just stared into his cup.

"If the Sentinels come up with a plan to help find them, wouldn't you want to be part of it?"

His head snapped up. "Of course."

"And if you weren't there to help, wouldn't you feel bad?"

He gave me a lopsided grin. "You have a certain way with words, and I think you're getting to know me pretty well." He stood. "I'll find someone to answer the phone and be over shortly."

I rose and gave him a quick hug. "I'm glad you're going to join us. I'll see you in a bit."

He hugged me in return, a longer one than I had given him. "Thanks, Kelly. Action of any kind will feel better than sitting here."

He left to find someone to help him, and I hurried to my Jeep and put Rex in the back. The drive to the inn was short. Rex went with me to Julie's room, where I retrieved his bed, went to the conference room, and put it next to where I'd be sitting. I didn't want him left alone. Rex settled in and I patted his head.

I taped a clean sheet of paper on the wall, took out our earlier charts, and hung those up as well. There might be something on them to help us with our new quest.

The group filtered in, along with Princess in her doggie purse. When Mary put her carrier down, she leapt out, and trotted over to Rex. They touched noses by way of introduction. That accomplished, she settled in the bed Mary had gotten from the closet.

We were ready to begin.

"Hi, everyone. Thanks for coming so quickly and at the spur-of-the-moment," I said.

The Professor nodded. "Of course, my dear. We have a major emergency on our hands."

Before we could continue any further, there was a knock on the door. I opened it to discover a disheveled Phil standing in front of me.

"I...I...saw you all arriving and thought maybe you had some news for me." Hope tried to peek out from his weary eyes.

For the second time in a short while, I had no comforting words to impart. "Phil, come in."

He stepped into the room. My lack of answer and the solemn looks from the others gave him his answer. "Nothing, right?"

The Professor patted the chair next to him. "Phil, my good man, sit down. Remember it's only been a number of hours since we learned of your predicament."

Phil plopped into the chair and ran his hand through his tight curls. "I know, but it seems like days."

"I understand, dear." Mary pushed a container of brownies in his direction. "Try one of these. I used mostly dark chocolate, which is good for you."

Phil sat, shoulders slumped, and ignored the proffered treat.

Gertie sat up straight and reached for her gavel. "We were about to start a meeting to decide what we can do to find three missing people, one of them being Michael Corrigan, the person helping you. Perhaps you'd like to join us and help out."

I quickly brought him up to speed.

His despondent look changed to one of concern. "Of course. I'll do anything I can."

Action suited him as it had done Scott. I could see a spark of the Phil I knew return to his eyes.

The gavel banged and the meeting started.

"I have news," I said. "It's official. Michael Corrigan's been kidnapped."

Gasps followed that announcement.

"Scott received a ransom demand," I continued. "He's going to join us in a while. There's also a strong suspicion the poachers are involved in the disappearance of the women and maybe Michael as well. The location where the car and tracks were found showed a lot of recent activity and is a prime location for the succulent they're after."

"So, what can we do to find these people?" Gertie asked.

We all stared at the empty white piece of paper on the wall.

Minutes passed.

Only silence.

This was a first.

Rudy cleared his throat. "Why don't we put down any new information we've collected on the poaching, if any, to get us thinking? Maybe we'll even find a connection. Kelly said there's a possibility the poachers are involved."

Rudy picked up a felt pen and went to the chart paper labeled "plant poachers" at the top.

Ivan chimed in with his usual booming voice. "Went to marina, talked to lots of people. More than usual number of motor boats past couple of months."

Rudy wrote the it down. "Yes. All manned by foreigners who speak very little English. There is one Caucasian man seen with them on occasion."

"Lots of activity at night. Vehicles come and go. Bags are loaded. Boats leave and others arrive," Ivan added.

Mary shook her head. "That certainly sounds like the poachers. I wonder why law enforcement hasn't done anything about it."

"Remember," Gertie said, "they can't move until they have a search warrant. To do that they need some tangible proof. That's what's been so frustrating for the Succulent Saviors."

"They could have seaweed or sea urchins in the bags, and those are legal to harvest," the Professor said.

"One of the garden club members saw the recovery of Eric's vehicle. It was very near where the poachers were arrested," Gertie said.

Rudy went to the new piece of chart paper on the wall. "Okay, what can we do to help find the missing people?"

The blank sheet of unmarred white still stared at us. We'd never been stumped like this before.

The silence lengthened. Thankfully, a knock disrupted the silent emptiness. This time Scott stood in the doorway, still in jeans and wearing the mud-spattered boots.

"Come on in," I said. "I've brought them up to date about the situation."

Mary hurried over and enveloped him in her plump arms then stepped back. "Michael's okay, honey. I'm sure of it."

"Thanks, Mary. I think he is for now." Scott settled in one of the empty chairs.

"Is there any possibility the women and Michael are together?" Gertie asked.

"We haven't heard anything to indicate that," Scott said. "But it's a possibility."

"We updated our poacher data. It seemed a good step since they might be involved," Rudy said.

Scott nodded. "I agree. The warden was adamant about warning people to be careful. I think the situation involving the poachers is very serious."

Rudy's pen was poised. He brought us back to the task at hand. "So, this is our sheet for next steps for the missing people. What are they?"

Again, we stared at the blank sheet. It reminded me of a field right after a snowfall with no tracks to mar its surface. I wanted the smooth, white surface to be trampled by ideas.

Phil had gone over to the coffee area and appeared to be searching amongst the cups and condiments.

"Phil, can I help you find something?" I asked.

"Today is a day for a sweet, rich, strong cup of coffee. Do you have any cream?"

"I'll get you some. The rest of us don't use it, so we don't put it out."

I headed for the kitchen, relieved to get away from the empty white paper waiting for our next steps. I retrieved a small ceramic pitcher from the cabinet and put it on the counter. I opened the refrigerator, took out a carton of cream, and filled the container. As I did so, a newspaper insert with the photo of a child at the bottom caught my eye.

"Missing" it read and an ad showed a picture of a young girl. My heart began to race.

Our next step had just been found.

Chapter 13

I put the carton away and picked up the cream I had poured and the ad. I rushed back to the meeting room. The group looked startled as I burst in. I held the insert up like a prize, which, in a sense, it was.

"I know what we can do! Make missing persons fliers."

There was a stunned moment of silence, then the Professor blinked a couple of times and said, "Brilliant, my dear."

Rudy wrote in bold, black letters wrote "To Do" on the once-blank chart paper and put fliers under it.

I put the paper on the table, and we all looked at the ad. I noticed, besides the photo, they had additional data like height, weight, date of birth, and date the girl went missing. A note mentioned she was diabetic.

The Professor stood. "I'm going to call my friend who has a print shop in Fort Peter and see what he can do for us." He stepped outside the room.

"Kelly," Mary said, "do you know if Julie, Cassie, or Michael had any medical issues?"

"Julie has seizures. I don't know about the others."

"Michael doesn't have any medical issues, to the best of my knowledge," Scott said. "Cassie's personal forms don't list any conditions."

"Let's make a list of what needs to go on the fliers," Gertie said. "Photos of the people for a start and a written description."

Rudy began making notes.

"I'd add photos of Cassie's car because it's so distinctive," I said. "I have the ones I sent the police."

Scott added, "I have ones of Michael, Cassie, and Julie. I can also provide the other information."

"How are we going to distribute them?" Rudy asked.

"I think we should create areas like the search and rescue people did," I said. "We could start with Redwood Cove and work outward. We assign people to the different sites."

"Count me in," Phil said. "I have a rental car and won't be doing much business for a while." He studied his hands. "My deliveries are locked in my van at the police station…and I don't think my clients want to talk to me at the moment."

Mary nudged the chocolate brownies she'd brought in his direction. "These will go well with your coffee. Your situation will get sorted out. You didn't do anything wrong, so we just have to find the person responsible."

The Professor came back in, wearing a big smile. "My friend is offering to stay tonight until the fliers are done. He isn't charging for his time and will only ask for the cost of the ink and the paper. He'll put them in a storage container at the side of the building so they'll stay dry until one of us can get them. He's going to make five thousand."

Scott raised his hand. "I can pick them up before dawn tomorrow and drop them off here. I don't expect I'll get much sleep tonight, and I can't help distribute them tomorrow because I'll be waiting for the money and to hear from the kidnappers."

The Professor twirled his pen. "That means we can start at sunrise tomorrow."

I frowned. "Is there any way we can do Redwood Cove tonight? Maybe make our own fliers just for the town? You know, the sooner the information is out there, the better."

"I don't see any reason why not," Scott said. "We have everything we need. I can access the photos from here. I can do it right now if I can borrow your computer. It won't look professional, but it'll do the job."

"Good news." I was already moving toward my quarters. "I can run them off on our copy machine." I stopped and turned. "Rex, stay."

The dog had started to rise, but he lay back down.

"Yah. We can put up tonight," Ivan said.

By the time I was back with my laptop, the group had started a list of places that had designated areas to post like markets, gas stations, and telephone poles. A note had been made to ask at other locations, like restaurants and drugstores.

I handed Scott my laptop, and he began putting the flier together.

"Let's keep track of where we post the fliers so we can take them down when they're home safe and sound," Mary said.

"Kelly," the Professor said, "can you find out what kind of medication Julie was taking? It might behoove us to contact local pharmacies and alert them to contact the police if a prescription for the drug shows up under Julie's name. We can split the task up between us."

After telling Rex to stay once again, I retrieved the pages Julie had given me. The Professor had gotten a phone book and was starting to write down drugstore names in his elegant, scholarly penmanship.

"Professor, that looks lovely, but why don't I just copy the pages you need on the copy machine?" I asked.

"Of course, my dear. That's a good idea." He capped his silver fountain pen. "Time is of the essence."

Rex knew the script now and stayed put while I went and made copies for all the Sentinels. When I returned, they put their heads together and divided up the businesses each would call. Walking a lot wasn't something Mary or Gertie could do, so they would make all the calls, except for ones where the men personally knew someone.

The Professor stood and made a rough map of the area on a new piece of chart paper, marking the towns of Redwood Cove and Fort Peter. "I suggest that Rudy, Ivan, and I take all of Fort Peter tomorrow. We'll split up so we can cover the area more quickly."

Phil stood, stretched, and walked to the chart. He pointed to the area south of Redwood Cove. "This is wine country I know well. I can work my way down the coast then take the main road into the valley."

"That leaves north and south of Fort Peter for me," I said.

"Good. We're set," the Professor said.

Gertie looked at me. "Kelly, while you were out, Mary and I talked. We'll come in with the Professor tomorrow and help Helen with the breakfast baskets. We've seen you doing them enough times we can lend a helping hand."

"But..." I started to object.

Helen could handle it on her own, but she'd already been asked to do more than usual with all that had been going on with meetings and the cooks in the kitchen.

"Thanks," I said. "I know she'll appreciate it."

"I'm done," Scott said.

I stood behind him and was impressed at the quality of the flier he'd put together in such a short time. I clicked on the print icon, using the wireless connection to the printer.

"I'll go make copies and be back shortly," I announced.

"We'll examine the list while you're gone and see if we can think of anything else to add," Gertie said.

"When was the last time you talked with Ned Blaine?" Deputy Stanton asked Joey.

"The last time I talked to him was also the last time I saw him—the town's salmon barbecue a couple of weeks ago. I helped with setup, and he asked me some questions for a newspaper article."

Stanton made some notes.

"Listen, Deputy Stanton, I know you know I didn't like the guy after breaking up our shoving match when Mom lost her job." Joey shrugged. "I didn't like the way he worded his article about the restaurant, which had people whispering and wondering if the food poisoning was Mom's fault, but that was a long time ago. I didn't kill the guy."

"Anything else, Deputy Stanton?" Elise asked. "If not, I'll put this food away and get on with my errands."

Stanton closed his notepad. "Nothing more for now, Elise."

She and Joey took care of the food, said their good-byes, and left.

"Time for me to go, too," Stanton said. "If you hear or see something you think might be helpful, give me a call."

He departed, a full day ahead of him.

Daniel and I looked at each other.

"Quite the turn of events," I said.

"Yes. Ned was pushy about our status but never malicious."

We sat in silence, lost in our thoughts.

Ned Blaine.

Dead.

Why did people murder? Sometimes to obtain what someone else had. What was so important that it meant taking a person's life? Or did a heated emotion get out of hand? Did the killer want to hide something and fear fueled the killing?

I shook my head and tried to refocus on the mundane, my to-dos for today.

I looked at the kitchen clock. "They're giving instructions for the contest today. Participants can meet and sign up with the different groups to take them for trial mushroom hunts. I want to go see what is offered and participate in some of the activities."

"I'm off on Ridley House errands," Daniel said, "but I plan on swinging by the event later. Some of my guests are participating in it. Maybe I'll see you there."

I went to my living quarters for a warm jacket. The fog hadn't lifted yet, and I knew the cold would knife through any fleece. I hadn't expected to be wearing my Wyoming down jacket in California. I still had a lot to learn about the area—but I was learning fast.

The small size of Redwood Cove leant itself to walking places, so I set off for the town center at a brisk pace. The meeting for the festival was outside the town hall, built in 1910. When I arrived, I found people milling about tables filled with coffee urns, doughnuts, and croissants, all the while smiling, eating, and sipping. I poured a cup of coffee and enjoyed the warmth of it in my hands. The fog began to lift and patches of bright blue sky appeared.

Roger Simmons stood at a podium. His faded blue jeans had a neat, sharp crease down the front, leading me to believe they'd been pressed. Ironed blue jeans? That was something I'd never seen in Wyoming. A tailored black sports coat covered his broad shoulders.

A waving hand from the Professor caught my eye as I surveyed the scene. The Professor, Timothy, Clarence, and canine Max of the golden curls occupied a place on the other side of the crowd. I wound my way through the happy festival-goers and joined them.

The Professor's bow tie matched his brown plaid cap and wool coat. Timothy and Clarence were dressed alike in black jeans and puffy coats, except for Clarence's bright red knit scarf and cap.

"Hi. Do you know what you're planning to sign up for today?" I asked them.

Clarence's grin seemed to stretch from ear to ear. "As many things as we can. The choices are such fun. Hiking, bicycling, horseback riding, paddling canoes, and off-roading are on our list in that order."

Timothy petted Max's head. "We've been told we go to a variety of different sites, and then we're on our own to search for mushrooms for a period of time. Clarence and I are going to do the activities together and then separate when we reach an area for searching. That'll allow us to share the fun of the traveling part together."

"That sounds like a great plan," I said.

I heard tapping on the microphone and turned my attention to Roger.

"Welcome, everyone," he said. "It's wonderful to see such a large turnout for our Mushroom Festival. Thank you for coming."

The crowd clapped. I noticed Peter off to my left.

"The purpose today is for you to see the ways you can go hunting tomorrow and try them out. The trips are short and we have two in the morning and three this afternoon. Tomorrow the excursions will be longer, with one in the morning and two in the afternoon. Sign-up information is on the table over there." He pointed to an area next to the building.

People turned and looked. A volunteer held up a stack of papers.

I took the flier to the copy machine and punched in five hundred. As the copies began to come, I realized we'd need a way to put them up. I went to the study and got a box of thumbtacks and a heavy-duty stapler. When I returned with the stack of fliers, I saw "contact churches and clubs for distribution" with Gertie and Mary in charge on one of the charts.

Rupert's name was also up there. He would be coming to pick up fliers to pass out to the Succulent Saviors. They'd take the area between Fort Peter and Redwood Cove. That left me only the north section.

I went over to the conference room schedule. It was clear for the rest of the week. "We can leave everything the way it is," I said. "You can work in here at any time. It'll make it easier for us to meet and share what we learn as we go along."

I remembered my grandfather talking about the war rooms in the military, and I'd heard the term used in businesses when they were putting together different strategies.

"It'll be our war room...our war against the kidnappers and the poachers."

"When we finish our areas, let's meet back here and see if there have been any new developments," the Professor said.

Scott rose. "I'll take some fliers tomorrow to distribute at the center."

Ivan, Rudy, and the Professor stood. "We'll be on our way to start putting these up."

The women bundled up and gathered their belongings, saying they'd see me in the morning. I walked out with Scott.

As we went down the hall, I asked, "Are you going to cancel tomorrow's welcoming event?"

"No," he replied. "Michael's worked long and hard to make this happen. He wouldn't want me to do that. I'll step in if he's not back by then."

I walked with him to the parking lot and waved as he left.

If he's not back by then.

I felt queasy. Julie. Cassie. Michael. All missing. One kidnapped for sure and probably the others. We'd kept an upbeat attitude during the meeting, talking about when they'd be back.

Night had snuck up while we'd been meeting. Somewhere in the pitch black three people were...where? With whom?

Would they ever return "safe and sound?"

Chapter 14

I tossed and turned all night. The alarm sounded, and I was grateful to call an end to the long hours. I peered outside and was greeted by a slight glimmer on the horizon. Dawn and time to distribute fliers. As I got ready, I wondered how our missing friends had fared.

Rex had remained settled in his bed. He'd climbed in after last night's walk and hadn't moved. His gaze followed me as I walked about. Maybe he figured I was his closest link back to Julie and wasn't going to let me out of his sight.

The dog and I moved down the hall. I opened the back door and found a tarp up against the wall of the inn. I pulled back a corner and found six boxes. One of them was opened. I looked in and saw fliers with open space at the top. This must have been the box that Scott had taken some from for the center.

I picked up a sheet and examined it. My breath caught in amazement. The printer had done a fantastic job. The photo colors were bright, clear, and eye-catching. The two women and Michael smiled at me from their publicity shots. The golden highlights on Julie's light brown hair shone, while Cassie's coal-black hair and creamy-white complexion made a stunning contrast. Strength and kindness emanated from Michael's eyes.

Tears welled in my eyes. I brushed them away.

They had to be all right. They just had to be.

Cassie's Beetle popped off the page with its colorful flowers on a bright green background. I was glad I had suggested adding pictures of it to the flier. If it was around to be seen, people would recognize it.

I folded the flier and slipped it into my pocket so I'd always have one with me. I put Rex in Helen's yard. It was very secure, and we had agreed it would be a good place to let him loose. I walked back to the inn. The brisk ocean breeze, with its tinge of salt, cleared the night's cobwebs from my brain but did nothing for the queasiness in my stomach. It remained.

I thought about Scott anxiously waiting to hear from the kidnappers, hoping Michael was still alive. This would be a difficult morning for him.

I walked up the porch steps and into the inn. Inhaling the smell of the freshly ground coffee as I scooped it into the filter, I appreciated the normalcy of the act. This was a time for one step after another, one task after another, and to keep going with the focus on finding our friends.

The coffee began to brew, and I went to get Rex. He waited patiently at the gate and walked quietly next to me back into the house. He situated himself in the same place he'd rested as Julie and Sebastian had been cooking. It seemed so, so long ago. Yet, it was only the day before yesterday. Not even forty-eight hours because I'd last been with them in the afternoon. One's sense of time could change so dramatically, depending on the circumstances.

I had gone out last night and gotten more thumbtacks so each person could have their own supply. Retrieving those, I put a couple of boxes on each case of fliers.

I made oatmeal for myself and fed Rex. I fixed a breakfast for Phil, along with extra coffee and a travel mug, and left it outside his room. The Professor texted the Silver Sentinels were on their way.

The sounds of a vehicle approaching alerted me to their arrival. I looked out the window and saw the Professor's vintage gold Mercedes sedan crawl into the driveway.

They all emerged as I opened the back door.

"Hi, honey, we're here to help," Mary called out in a quiet voice so as not to disturb our guests.

I'd explained the situation to Helen the night before. She had smiled and said she could handle the baskets but was happy for the assistance. At some level, I think we both knew we were doing it for them. They wanted to help, feel like they were contributing. She had also offered to take care of Rex while I distributed fliers.

"Do any of you want coffee?" I asked.

The guys all lifted travel mugs to let me know they were covered.

"Later, dear," Mary said.

Helen emerged from her cottage and joined us on the porch. She picked up one of the fliers. "These turned out first-rate. I hope they do the trick."

"We do too," I said.

"I'll go start the breakfast baskets." She entered the inn.

Out of the corner of my eye, I saw Phil descending the stairs from his building. One hand was shoved in his left jeans' pocket; the other one gripped the travel mug I'd left for him. He wore a wool cap and a heavy maroon fleece, as well as sturdy walking shoes. Not his usual wine merchant attire of neat black slacks and colorful, embroidered vests.

When he joined us, I noticed he'd not bothered to shave. Maybe he figured he'd just go with his "bad boy" image and skip it.

"Good morning, everyone," he said. "Kelly, thanks for the extra coffee and the travel cup. Much appreciated." He glanced at the boxes. "I'll go get my rental car."

Ivan walked up the steps and picked up one of the cases. He went down and put it in the trunk of the Mercedes. I started to pick one up then stopped. It was much heavier than I realized.

"Wait," Ivan called out. "I get for you."

He picked up a box, and we walked together to my Jeep. I unlocked it, and he placed it behind the driver's seat. I had my supplies for the day and, hopefully, the tools to bring my friends home.

Phil parked next to my Jeep and got a box of fliers. Ivan loaded another two boxes into the Professor's car. The partially empty one was left for Rupert. He didn't have as much territory to cover.

The Professor addressed me. "My friend said he'd print out more at any time if we need them. He's making it a priority."

Another example of the community coming together in a time of need. I'd spent a brief time in some big cities, where people could live next door to each other for years and not know their neighbor's name. This is the life I wanted. People caring about other people…whether they knew them or not.

"When we get back," the Professor said, "let's put whatever we have left over here." He pointed to the tarp. "That way we can keep track of how many we have and they're available if any of us need more."

"We have news," Ivan announced.

Rudy nodded. "We spent the night on the *Nadia* and took some evening strolls. We observed the activities we'd been told about."

"Yah, and talk to Joe."

Joe. Owner of the bait store. I'd met him on my first visit to the brothers' boat. The missing front tooth created a slight lisp but didn't mar his broad smile. His comfortable bib overalls suited him well as he surveyed the action around him, sometimes using the binoculars he kept next to his rocking chair.

"He's been taking notes," Rudy said, "to the extent of writing down license plate numbers when he could. Joe's been sharing them with the wardens who visit frequently. We're going to go over later and get the information from him. We'll have that to add to our charts."

"Joe said one of bags dumped out in parking lot. Seaweed," Ivan said.

Rudy nodded. "Joe suspects they wanted to hide what they were really doing."

"Interesting…and smart," the Professor said. "It could've been a warning to law enforcement they needed to have concrete proof before getting a search warrant."

"We're off to help Helen," Gertie said. "Then we'll make phone calls from the war room."

Her eyes glinted as she said this. I got the feeling she liked the name and concept for what the conference room had become.

"Yes," Mary said. "The charts will all be updated with anything new when you return."

Gertie and Mary walked up the back steps. They stopped and each took a handful of fliers then went in. We bid each other goodbye, got in our vehicles, and headed out to our designated areas. I decided to start at the far end of my territory. I drove past Fort Peter to the small town of Running Creek. After posting at the only local market and being directed to a community announcement board, I went to a coffee shop. Judging by the number of cars outside, a popular one.

I approached a woman wearing a white apron, her bleached blond hair pulled back in a ponytail, wiping down a counter. I explained what had happened and asked if I could put up a flier.

"Of course. How dreadful to have your friends missing. I hope they're okay."

So do I.

The scenario repeated itself. No one turned me down. Everyone offered their condolences and their well wishes. After an hour, I was tired. After two hours, I was exhausted. It was going to be a long day. Sipping my lukewarm coffee didn't help.

Four hours later I had completed my area. I headed back to Redwood Cove, passing the string of budget hotels lining the highway in Fort Peter that appeared predominanatly in the Succulent Saviors' photos. Were Michael and the two women being held in one of those dingy rooms?

Ten minutes into the drive to Redwood Cove B & B, Cassie's one-of-a-kind vehicle zipped by me, traveling in the opposite direction. Cassie was at the wheel. I gasped, not believing my eyes. I did a quick turn around at the next vista point. I hit the gas hard to catch up. I caught a glimpse of her exiting the road. I slowed as I neared where she had turned in. A large sign said "Cabins for Rent."

Questions raced through my mind. Did Cassie have something to do with Julie's disappearance? Had she kidnapped her for some reason? Or worse, hurt her? Was there jealousy involved around the cooking event? Did she fear people might think Julie was the better chef? Did she have anything to do with Michael's kidnapping and the ransom demand?

Slowing down, I turned and bumped down a gravel road. A slight hint of dust indicated a vehicle's recent passing. I spotted Cassie getting out of her VW bug in front of a rustic cabin and pulled over behind a stand of trees. She clutched a bag with her left arm and held keys in her right hand. Cassie unlocked the building's door, nudged it open with her knee, and disappeared from sight as she entered the structure.

I got out of my car, crouching low, and peeked inside through one of the windows. Cassie was unloading groceries. A kitchen table had a yellow and white striped vinyl tablecloth that somewhat matched the faded laminate counters. The brown linoleum would conceal a magnitude of stains.

A closed door lead to another room. I had no way of knowing if anyone was in there.

I bent down and took a moment to think about my next move. Should I check to see if there was a way to see into the other room or confront Cassie? Another quick look inside showed me she had finished unloading the groceries, folded the bag, and had poured herself a soda. Her fleece rested over a chair's arm. She sat at a table reading a magazine. Cassie seemed to be settling in.

I made my way quickly around the cabin. A hint of mold tinged the dank air. The room had a window, albeit a dirty one. However, what kept me from seeing inside was the closed curtain. I went back to my original position and peered in.

Cassie was wearing leggings with a tank top. There was no way she could conceal a weapon. She might have an accomplice, but I figured odds were that person would've come forward when she had returned.

I shifted to crane my neck to see if there was anything else in the room that might provide me with answers. A twig snapped under my foot, and Cassie's head jerked up.

I ducked as soon as the sound happened. I remained motionless, not sure if she would come out or go back to what she was doing. I tried to still my racing heart and the pulse that pounded in my ears. I knew she couldn't hear it, but I sure could. When a few moments had passed and she hadn't come out, I risked another look inside.

I saw her open the door to the room I hadn't been able to see into. She entered it, and the edge of a bed appeared, but nothing more. No one came out. I didn't think anyone was there and decided to risk a confrontation.

Cassie hadn't completely closed the front door to the cabin. I went to the entryway of the cabin and knocked. Cassie came out of the room and stopped. A bewildered look of surprise was quickly replaced by one of anger.

"What are you doing here? How did you know how to find me?" she demanded.

"Where's Julie?"

"What do you mean 'Where's Julie?' She's preparing for the cooking event." Confusion now filled her features.

"No, she's not. She's missing. We think she's been kidnapped."

"No...no..." Fear contorted Cassie's features. "That can't be. She was fine when I left her."

"You were supposed to stay together."

"I...I...know, but she had Rex. I figured she'd be safe." Cassie sat abruptly on one of the dining room chairs.

"You figured wrong. Her vehicle was found with Rex in it and no sign of her."

I pulled the flier from my pocket, unfolded it, and held it out to Cassie.

She shook her head. "No...no." Tears flowed down Cassie's face. "She's my best friend. I let her down. It's my fault something has happened." She buried her face in her hands and sobbed.

I pulled a chair from the table, sat in front of her, and rested my hands on my thighs. "Cassie, pull yourself together. Tell me what happened. Maybe there's something you know that can help the police find her."

Cassie took a deep breath and straightened up. She pulled some tissues from a box on the table.

She looked at me with red, swollen eyes. "I followed her to the place we'd agreed to forage." Cassie began to shred the tissues in her hands. "She started to walk and I stopped her, said I wanted to talk. We got in my Beetle, and I told her I wanted some time away from my husband to sort out what to do." She stopped talking.

"What did you mean by that?" I urged her on.

"I love Ian deeply, but his jealousy has gotten out of hand. We argue constantly. He's come close to threatening some of my coworkers. I can't continue like this."

Again, silence. Impatience warred with my compassion. Impatience won.

"Cassie, then what? We need to get to what happened as quickly as possible and contact the police. It might help find Julie."

She nodded. "Of course. I'm being selfish and that is what led to this situation. I put myself first. I wanted time to myself to think through what I wanted to do." She burst into tears again, using what was left of the tissues to wipe her eyes. "I told Julie I wanted to disappear for a couple of days. She said go for it and she understood. So, I came here."

Cassie leaned forward and grabbed my hands. "I never, for an instant, would have left her alone if I thought she was in danger."

I gave her hands a squeeze. "I believe you. What you need to do now is call the police and tell them where you and Julie parted company. It might have been where they found her vehicle, or the car might have been moved."

"Of course. I don't have cell service here, but I'll go to the registration building."

Her shoulders heaved with sobs as she stumbled toward the office.

One person found, two still missing, to the best of my knowledge. Was Michael safely back with Scott? Did he know anything about Julie? And Cassie…was she telling the truth? Or did she have something to do with Julie's disappearance and maybe even Michael's?

Chapter 15

I sat on one of the shabby wooden kitchen chairs and didn't have long to wait for Cassie to return. I could see her approaching through the back window and wondered how she'd gotten away without being seen.

She opened the door. "The police want to see me as soon as possible. I'm supposed to meet them at the community center and take them to where Julie and I parted company to be sure that's the same place her car was... just like you said. I...I checked out of here. I want to be in town helping to find Julie as much as I can."

The tears had stopped streaming, but her eyes remained red and swollen. She opened the grocery bag she'd just emptied and began filling it with the food she'd put away.

I stood. "Let me do that. You can work on getting your things together."

"Thanks. I don't have much. It won't take long."

She disappeared into the bedroom and came out with a duffel bag. Working her way around the room, she picked up her belongings and stuffed them into the black canvas tote.

This was a good time to ask her the question that had been bothering me. "Cassie, no one at the community center saw you drive out. How did you manage that?"

"There was a bit of a traffic jam the day the chefs arrived for the introductory meeting. One of the veterans pulled me aside and told me about a road through the trees that circumvents that area. At one point I could take a left and pull into the main parking lot or a right and head straight out for the main road." She crammed a fleece into the now-bulging duffel. "You know which way I went. There was a brief moment when Ian would've been able to see me, but I decided to take the chance."

The grocery bag was full. "Is your car unlocked? I'll take this out."

She opened the door. "Yeah. I'll come with you and put this tote away."

I opened the passenger side door and placed the food on the floor.

On our way back to the cabin, I asked, "Did anyone else know you were doing this?"

She shook her head. "I was so scared of Ian finding out, I didn't talk to anyone but Julie."

"Weren't you worried about losing your job?"

"Not really. I've known the restaurant owner for years. He's been hinting that Ian needed to be reined in. I felt he'd be supportive of my trying to work it out." She shrugged. "And if he fired me, I'm fortunate enough to be well respected in the culinary community, and I don't think I would've had any trouble getting another position."

She disappeared into the bedroom again and came out with a black coat draped over one arm. "That's it." Cassie put the cabin keys on the table. "This place served its purpose in terms of being remote and isolated, giving me a good hiding place, but I can't say as I'll miss it."

I stood next to her vehicle as she got in. "Now what?"

"Like I said, do everything I can to help find Julie."

"What about Ian? Are you afraid of him? Do you think he might hurt you?"

She shook her head. "He's more likely to hurt himself, like he did before."

"I think you should tell the police about him. They're going to ask you why you ran away. I hope you'll give them the whole story."

"You're right." She sighed. "I don't know how everything got so messed up."

"If it helps any, Ian and I talked. He really loves you and knows he's creating problems. He wants to change."

"I know he does...but I don't know if he can."

Cassie started her engine and gave me a wave. I returned to my Jeep and continued my drive home. I knew where cell phone service started on the way back to Redwood Cove and pulled off the road to call Scott when I reached it. I used his cell phone number so the center lines stayed open.

"Kelly," Scott said after the first ring. "I haven't heard from the kidnappers. Nothing. The money's here." Fear and anxiety mingled in his voice.

I looked at my watch. "It's not quite noon. They said they'd call in the morning. There's still time."

"What if Michael is no longer alive? What if he tried to escape and they killed him?"

My heart went out to him. "Scott, there could be any number of reasons why they haven't called. Maybe the police were getting close to where they were hiding and they had to make a run for it. Maybe they ended up where there is no phone service. Maybe they're playing a game with you in order to ask for more money."

I heard him exhale. "You're right. Going to the worst-case scenario doesn't help. Thanks for all the other possible reasons why they haven't called."

"One bit of good news. I found Cassie." I told him what had transpired. "She should be at the center shortly."

"A positive note helps," he said.

"Here's another maybe. Maybe Michael escaped and he's trying to get to some place where he can contact the police."

"I like that one, too," Scott said. "I know the police would get in touch with me as soon as they heard from him. Extra officers have been put here to help guard the money. Having a million in cash sitting in a truck isn't something to make the area's law enforcement happy." The edge of pain in his voice had dissipated, leaving him sounding weary.

"Hang in there, Scott."

"I will. There's not much else I can do."

"Why don't you write down some more 'maybe' scenarios? It'll be interesting to see which one is correct when Michael returns."

"I'll think about it...and thanks for keeping 'when' as part of the conversation."

Someone in the background called his name.

"I'll call you later if I don't hear from you," I said.

"Okay."

I heard him tell the person he'd be right there.

"And, Kelly, please be careful. I know you are, but you've had some close calls, and we don't know who we're dealing with or how many of them there are."

"You're right, Scott. Nothing rash on my part."

Scott worried about me and the Silver Sentinels getting hurt while investigating. It was because he cared about us, but it had caused some conflicts in the past.

We ended the call, and I took a moment to text the Sentinels and Helen with the news about Cassie. I continued on to the inn. A flasy, bright red sports car parked in the lot reminded me Michael's guests were arriving today. They'd be staying at various inns and resorts in the area. I parked next to the vehicle. I didn't know much about cars, but I knew the rearing yellow horse on the fender identified it as a Ferrari.

When I entered the workroom, Rex greeted me with a wildly wagging tail. He was probably hoping I had Julie with me.

Helen turned from where she was working at the counter. "Good news about Cassie."

"I agree. How did Rex do?"

"He was very well-behaved. He and Fred had some playtime as well."

"Thanks for taking care of him."

"You're welcome."

I decided to check the war room to see if there was any news. "Come on, Rex."

He trotted to my side, and we went to the conference room.

A chart had been added and labeled, "message board." "Twelve fifteen Gertie taking fliers to quilting club" had been written on it. Underneath the same time, "Mary taking fliers to church meeting" had been added. A nice touch. There was nothing about the others, so I figured they were still distributing the fliers.

I stared at our charts and the easel with the photos of the poachers. I walked over to it. I'd passed the same buildings not long ago.

Rex leaned against me, and I patted him. "Any ideas, fella, about what we can do next to find your mom?"

He leaned harder, but no thoughts from the doggie world transferred from his head to mine. I studied the photos. In some there were a few vehicles scattered through parking lots adjacent to the Pacific Ocean cliffs. In others, dirty vans in front of cheap motels were lined up one after another.

Wait. I had a thought. Maybe Rex *was* getting through to me.

He wasn't a trained tracker, but I was sure he'd let me know if he smelled Julie. A casual walk by the vans and his actions would let me know if she'd been there. Excitement coursed through me. It wouldn't be dangerous. It was broad daylight and the motels were off of a well-traveled highway. I wouldn't go near the doors to the rooms, and I'd check to be sure bystanders were present to dissuade anyone with bad intentions from approaching me.

I went to the area where I'd left the papers Gertie had handed out. I picked up the list of hotels with the license plate numbers of the vehicles the Succulent Saviors were suspicious of, along with a brief description. They were all white rental vans or panel trucks. Someone had arranged the list of motels geographically, so it would be easy to go down the line.

Pausing, I decided to take a photo of the list. My plan was to casually walk Rex by the vehicles to see if he reacted. Pulling out a piece of paper and checking it as I stared at a license plate might alarm someone. Looking at my phone, on the other hand, wouldn't raise an eyebrow.

"Come on, Rex, it's time for you to go to work."

I trotted to my rooms with him on my heels. I took a half a leftover sandwich from the refrigerator. Getting tired from lack of food wouldn't help the situation. As I ate, I thought about what I needed to take with me. I'd want my good camera with the serious zoom capabilities for sure. A notepad in case I wanted to make notes and the tourist map of Fort Peter to help find the motels rounded out my list.

A black wool cap to cover my red hair would be a smart choice. I didn't want to stand out in any way. I finished my food and filled one of my water bottles with a jug of cold water in the refrigerator. My jacket was still in the car from this morning.

Rex and I headed out of the room.

I put him in the back of my Jeep, got in, and placed the map, camera, and notepad on the passenger seat. I took my binoculars out of the glove box then drove back the way I'd just come. The motels occupied a strip along the highway not too far from each other. They were the cheapest rooms in town as they fronted a busy road and were on the shabby side. There was no mistaking them for quaint inns or resorts.

I decided I'd start my search at motels with vans parked out front. I slowed as I neared the first motel on my list. There were no vans. If necessary, I'd come back and stake the place out when I finished with the other sites.

I had better luck at the next location. I spotted a dirty, white van and a panel truck. There was a busy restaurant adjacent to the strip of rooms, with a steady stream of customers going in and out. I parked there, put Rex on a leash, and sauntered toward a patch of lawn on the far side of the motel. Just a person walking her dog. I paused at the van for a moment and pretended to search for something in my purse to give Rex time to sniff around. As I did so, I checked the license plate number on my phone. It was one of the ones listed.

Rex didn't need a command to check the vehicle out. His doggie ways were always about checking out new smells. He finished with the back of the van, moved around the side a bit, then on to the next vehicle. Nothing at the first stop.

The panel truck was next. It was on my list as well, but Rex said, "nothing there" by coming back to my side. I finished my trip to the grassy area to complete the charade then back to my Jeep.

No vehicles at the next stop. I spied a van at the next motel and parked half a block away. It was midmorning and people were checking out. I meandered by the vehicles parked in front of the rooms, gazing occasionally at the beautiful blue sky. A tourist enjoying a walk…though I knew there were much better places for strolling. Hopefully, the poachers didn't. I repeated the same routine with the new vehicle. Rex had no interest.

Three places to go. Parking wasn't as easy at the next site, where I could see a van and a couple of rusted trucks in front of several rooms. There was street parking next to the end of the row. Rex and I exited and the smell of something rotten hit me as I passed a dumpster. I rounded it and walked over a bunch of discarded cigarette butts.

I hesitated, searching for some bystanders. Through the office window, I saw a clerk at the counter. He would have to do for backup. I did the same stroll, slowed as I got to the van, and verified it was on the list. Rex tugged at his leash and began whining. He got on his hind legs and pawed at the back of the vehicle.

Bingo.

Pay dirt.

My heart raced.

I believed Julie had been in the van.

Rex's whines got louder. I pulled him around and hurried back to my Jeep. He resisted and began to fight the leash, barking. I was worried he'd be heard and had no time to persuade him to be quiet. I picked him up, no easy feat with a squirming, approximately thirty-pound dog, and carried him to the Jeep. I put him down at the back of the car, opened the gate, picked him up again, put him in the back, and quickly closed the door.

Did I call Stanton or 911? I had no proof Julie was in there. Stanton knew the situation. Luckily, he answered after the first ring.

"Deputy Stanton, I have every reason to believe Julie has been in a van parked at the Good Night Motel in Fort Peter. She might be in one of the rooms right now."

"What leads you to believe this, Ms. Jackson?"

"I walked her service dog by the van, and he went crazy with excitement and began whining. Can you get a search warrant?"

"Is he a trained search dog? If not, there could have been something tasty to eat in that van."

"No, he's not trained to the best of my knowledge. But if you'd seen how he reacted, I believe you'd agree with me."

"I don't want to start an official request based on the dog's reaction. However, I'll run it by the district attorney and see what he has to say."

"Thanks, Deputy Stanton."

"Uh…Ms. Jackson, how is it you happened to be at the motel walking the dog by that van?"

Busted. He didn't like it when the Silver Sentinels and I were investigating.

"Well, it's like this…" I went on to tell him about the list from the Succulent Saviors of the suspected poachers and what my plan was.

"Let me get this straight. You're at a low-rent hotel checking for suspected poachers and possible kidnappers. Do I have that right?"

The way he said it made my rationale for being safe sound flimsy.

"Yes…but I checked to be sure other people were around, and I never got near the doors of the rooms."

His sigh was one I'd heard a number of times before. "I'm sending over an officer to watch the place while I check on the search warrant. If you're not gone when he gets there, he'll ask you to leave."

"Okay, Deputy Stanton."

He hung up without a goodbye.

I decided not to leave until the policeman arrived in case there was any activity around the vehicle. I settled back in the driver's seat, turned on the radio to cover Rex's continued complaining, and picked up the town map I'd put on the seat, striving to appear as if I was waiting for a friend. As I pretended to be relaxed and casual, the whole time my heart pounded.

Are Michael and Julie in there?

No sooner had I had that thought than the door to the room in front of the van opened. An Asian man came out, unlocked the back of the van, and opened the doors. He had two large canvas bags over his shoulder, and he tossed those inside the vehicle. I grabbed my camera and zoomed in. He had a sparse black beard that didn't completely cover the pockmarks on his face. I took several photos, keeping as low as I could.

He went to the driver's side and tugged on the handle. It didn't budge. He yanked it hard, and it opened. He got in and closed the door. The back had been left ajar. A moment later, a second man came out with more bags, only these were clearly full. This man was Asian as well, with a cap pulled down over his face and wearing a puffy olive-green jacket and stained tan trousers. I photographed him but couldn't get a good shot of his face.

He returned to the room then came out holding Michael Corrigan by the arm.

Michael was alive! Relief flooded through me.

I could see Michael's arms were stretched behind him, his hands out of sight. I figured they were tied. A jacket had been placed over his shoulders to conceal his hands.

As soon as I saw Michael, I put down my camera, grabbed my phone, and dialed Stanton.

It took him several rings to answer. "No need for a search warrant," I said. "A man just led Michael out of the motel."

"I'm on my way."

As I put the phone in the holder I'd installed on the dashboard, the man gestured with his head for Michael to enter the vehicle and he got in. I had a clear look at the man's face as he did so. It was moon-shaped, and he had puffy cheeks. The man left and returned with Julie.

Both were okay!

She, too, had her hands out of sight behind a sweater. Julie entered the van, the man closed the door, and got in on the passenger's side.

The van backed out and turned left onto the main road.

I pushed the button to call Stanton and put the phone on speaker as I pulled out behind them. "They're going south on the highway. They have Julie, too. I'll be out of cell phone range soon. I'm following them." I ended the communication before he could order me to stay put.

The van went a short distance out of town before turning off on a gravel road with signs indicating beach access. I passed the turn-off so they wouldn't see me behind them. I did a U-turn as soon as I could and went down the same road. The road forked, with one arm indicating the beach and the other a vista point. A slight dust cloud heading toward the viewing area made me choose that path.

I saw the van parked in a clearing, which sloped toward the ocean, and pulled in behind a thick stand of redwoods on a hill above the area. The two men with large canvas sacks over their shoulders walked off toward the rocky cliffs. I searched in my purse for my pocketknife. I found it and slipped it into my jacket. I waited a few minutes then got out. I ran down to the van and opened the back of it.

Julie and Michael, bound and gagged, were sitting there. Their feet had been tied to a ring in the floor. Their eyes widened when they saw me. I jumped in and pulled out my knife. I cut off Julie's gag and then Michael's.

"Kelly, thank goodness you found us," Julie said.

"I second that," Michael added.

I began to work on Julie's cord-tied hands. The van was parked facing downward on a slope. I felt it inch forward ever so slightly.

"Kelly, they've been having trouble with the handbrake. Give me the knife, and I'll cut Julie loose and then she can free me. You need to keep the vehicle from rolling."

Given there was a cliff ahead of us, I couldn't agree more. I gave him the knife and Julie turned around so Michael could work at cutting the cords. Not an easy task, given his hands were behind his back. Fortunately, the men hadn't made them super tight. They were taut enough to keep them bound, but the knife could be worked carefully through the rope without causing an injury.

I made my way to the driver's seat just as the van began to move ahead again. I stomped on the brake pedal. I kept my foot on it while I pulled hard on the handbrake. The vehicle stopped. I released my hold on the brake pedal and turned to address Michael and Julie. The van started forward again. We'd been still for only a couple of seconds.

I hit the brake again with my foot. I looked over my shoulder and saw Michael cutting the last of the rope binding their feet.

"You two run for it. My Jeep is straight up the hill. I'll go out the side door."

They jumped out the back and began running. I looked forward and saw the frightening cliff ahead. I pulled hard on the handbrake then took my foot off the brake pedal. The van continued to inch forward. I pulled the door handle on the driver's side. No response. The rusty hinges were unwilling to respond.

I stomped on the brake and the vehicle stopped again. I tried rolling down the window, but it was jammed. I tried the door again, but no luck. I didn't have the strength I needed in the position I was in to force it open. I glanced to the passenger side. There was nothing to say that door would be any better.

The van began to creep forward. Now even my foot on the brake wasn't enough to hold it. If it kept moving, I'd be going over the cliff.

Fear gripped me as I saw the drop-off ahead.

Chapter 16

I saw several large trees off to my left. I took a deep breath, took my foot off the brake, and pulled hard on the steering wheel in the hopes of crashing the van into them to stop it. The vehicle turned and pointed to where I was aiming. I stomped on the brake to slow it down while I tried to solve how to get out of the van.

I looked in the rearview mirror and saw the back doors had closed. Would they stick like the driver's door? They hadn't when I'd opened them earlier. Going out the back was my best bet, and I needed to do it now before the men came back and the van crashed.

Releasing the brake, I turned, bolted to the back of the van, and pushed one of the doors open. I jumped out and rolled as I tripped and fell. Years of being thrown from horses had perfected this movement. A loud bang and the tinkle of glass told me I'd succeeded in hitting my target.

I saw Michael and Julie in the distance and ran hard to catch up. Suddenly, Julie sank to her knees and then went down on the ground. I saw her body began to convulse. When I reached them, her face had begun to twitch. Michael picked her up.

She must be having a seizure.

"I'll get the Jeep and come back for you," I shouted.

I sprinted ahead as Michael carried Julie as fast as he could, without jarring her too much. Just as I reached the Jeep, a loud yell alerted me the men had discovered their van and seen us. I got in my Jeep and started it. One of the men was in the van trying to get it going. I could hear the engine turning over. The other one ran toward us. I didn't know if he had a weapon and had no desire to find out.

I hit the gas then slammed on the brakes as I reached Michael and Julie. I jumped out and opened the back door. Michael sat on the edge of the seat and scooted in, holding Julie on her side. Her arms and legs jerked repeatedly.

As soon as he was in, I closed the door, got in the Jeep, and spun it around. I headed up the hill, quickly putting the poacher behind us. A glance in the rearview mirror showed their van hadn't moved.

I also noticed Michael adjust the hold he had on Julie. "Go straight to the hospital. It's on Third Street. You turn right at the tourist information building."

I knew where he was talking about. One of the requirements of new managers was to become familiar with important locations in the area.

Michael put his hand out over the seat. "Let me have your phone. I'll call the police as soon as I have a signal."

I pulled it out of the holder and handed it to him. "Try Stanton first. He knows what's going on, and it will save time explaining what's happened."

"Good idea. I'll get his number ready."

We'd been ignoring Rex's whines during all the excitement, so he decided to start barking.

"Rex, quiet," I said. "Julie doesn't need to be worrying about you right now."

It was almost as if he understood. He quieted down, sat, and stared intently at his owner from behind the wire barrier.

I reached the highway and saw a restaurant. I looked at Michael in the mirror. "Do you want me to stop and use their landline phone to call for help?"

He frowned and looked at the convulsing woman in his arms. "No. Let's get her to the hospital. It's only a short distance."

I put my hand on the horn and kept it there, alerting people to our speeding vehicle. As we neared town, I heard Michael reach Stanton. He got the deputy up to speed about what had happened, where the van had crashed, and where we were headed. He tossed my phone back into the front seat.

"A police car is on the way to lead us to the hospital."

As he said that, flashing lights appeared ahead of us. A squad car made a U-turn and pulled in front of us, sirens blaring. I took my hand off the horn, grateful for the escort. When we reached the hospital, a team was waiting for us. A police car was there as well.

I jumped out and opened the back door. I shuddered as I caught the vacant stare in Julie's eyes. They gently helped remove her from the back seat and raced her inside on a gurney. Michael followed them in. Rex began to howl.

I reached through the wire and scratched his neck. "Everything's going to be okay. You'll be with her soon."

He quieted down and curled up on the floor with a dejected look on his face. I returned to the driver's seat.

Michael came out and joined me in the front seat. "Stanton wants us to meet him at the motel where we were being held."

I headed for the motel, where all the chase had started. Michael rubbed his face with his hands, as if to wipe away the tiredness I saw in his red eyes and the frown lines marring his unshaven face.

"Are you okay?" I asked.

He nodded. "Not an afternoon, night, and morning I ever want to experience again, but not anything a good rest won't take care of."

I parked in the same spot I'd been in earlier. The cool weather, often foggy skies, and an abundance of trees made finding safe places to leave a dog in a car an easy task. Rex would be fine here.

"You go ahead," I said. "I want to call Scott. I'll catch up with you."

Michael got out and headed for the room where he'd been held captive.

I phoned Scott. "Corrigan and Julie are safe. We're in Fort Peter and at the motel where they were held. I'll explain more later."

"What's the name of the hotel? I'll be there as fast as I can."

I gave it to him and we both hung up.

No time for niceties from either of us.

I texted the Sentinels and Helen an update then walked to the room and looked in. It was dingy, with two double beds and a cot shoved against the closet. Officers, along with Warden Rodriguez, were inventorying and photographing the contents of the room. A "Do Not Disturb" sign dangled from the doorknob.

Several canvas bags rested in one corner. They'd been opened, and I could see numerous succulents crowded in on top of each other.

Stanton approached us and stuck out his hand to Michael. "Good to see you safe and sound."

"Glad to be that way," Michael replied. "Can I take my stuff and Julie's?" He pointed to a pile on the floor, which had a wallet, cell phone, a purse, and other items.

"Let me be sure we have what we need for the report and photos."

Stanton talked to one of the officers and returned. "Yes, you can take them. Now, I'd like to hear what happened."

Michael nodded. "Let's go outside. I've had enough of this room."

We went out and Stanton pointed to a table and some chairs at the end of the string of rooms.

"We can sit there," the officer said.

"I'd like Kelly to join us, if possible. She can be my spokesperson while I get some rest this afternoon," Michael said.

"That's your call. No reason to repeat the story twice."

The rusted wrought iron chairs and cracked vinyl seats didn't look comfortable, but they would suffice. I removed the overflowing ashtray and placed it on the ground next to a fence then sat next to Michael. Stanton took out his notebook and the story began.

Michael leaned back. "I came around a corner when I was searching for Julie and caught the poachers in the act of digging up plants. One of them had a knife and immediately confronted me. I believe I could've gotten away, but then another one came up and showed me a photo of Julie. She was bound and gagged. He said if I didn't come with them, they'd hurt her."

The queasy feeling I had experienced earlier came back.

"I figured I might have a chance to find a way for both of us to escape. I was also concerned about her having seizures and wanted to be there to help if possible. I let them tie me up with no resistance. That's when they drove me to this place." He looked around at the litter-strewn parking lot. "I managed to drop a ticket stub without them noticing thinking it might help you piece together what happened."

"Scott found it. That and your footprints put you on our missing person's list." Stanton paused in his note taking. "I would've done the same to help the young woman." He poised his pen, ready to go on. "How many were there?"

"Two were poaching and one was here with Julie. They were of Asian descent. The one who showed me the photo of Julie speaks English and whatever language the poachers speak. He's Caucasian and dropped in several times."

Stanton stopped writing. "He was probably what we call a handler. We have them with abalone poachers as well. Teams are brought in to do the stealing, and the handler organizes transportation, lodging, etcetera…as well as bail and fines if they get caught."

Michael nodded. "His plan was pretty clever, actually. He made it clear if I got away, Julie would pay, and vice versa. We were collateral for each other." Michael heaved a sigh. "He actually was quite polite, almost apologetic. He explained the plants would set the poachers up comfortably for the rest of their lives in China. He planned to disappear with his cut, which would allow him to live very well for years to come. They were about to quit poaching and leave. Three of their group had been arrested recently, and they didn't want anything or anyone else to mess up their plans. They assured us if we didn't try to escape, we'd be let free unharmed."

"What about the ransom request?" Stanton asked.

"Again, another smart move. He used it as a decoy. They'd get what they needed from the poaching if they could get the plants out of the country, along with themselves."

A black Mercedes pulled into the parking lot and screeched to a halt. Scott got out and hurried toward us.

Michael stood and the two clasped each other. Scott resembled Michael in terms of his tired look and not his usual clean-shaven self.

"Glad you're okay, Michael."

"I'm sure you've been holding down the fort just fine, Scott."

Their affection for each other was clear.

Stanton acknowledged Scott with a nod. "Join us. Michael is catching us up on what happened. When he finishes, Kelly can fill you in on what you missed."

Scott pulled out a wobbly chair and sat. "Thanks."

Stanton's phone buzzed. "Stanton here." He listened for a minute. "Good news. Thanks."

The words "good news" had us all looking at him expectantly.

"Julie's going to be fine. They want to keep her a while longer. I have two of my men there. I wasn't sure what the situation was and wanted them there for protection. When she feels up to it, they'll get a statement from her and let me know."

Michael put his arms over his head, clasped his hands, and stretched. He looked at me. "Kelly, how did you find us?"

Stanton made a funny sound and tossed his pen on the table.

I filled Michael in on what had happened.

Scott frowned and shook his head.

"Yep," Michael said. "I made a good choice when I hired a Wyoming cowgirl."

We chuckled and the tension I'd seen building in Scott via frowns appeared to lessen.

Michael squeezed my hand. "You're the heroine of the day, for sure. Thank you for rescuing us. Those words seem insufficient, but they do say it all."

Warden Rodriguez came out and sat in the last chair. "We have all the evidence we need to prosecute these men for poaching when we catch them."

"I'm guessing they're leaving tonight," Michael said. "The man you believe is their handler paid the hotel bill today. He placed it on top of a bureau, and I got a chance to see it. They have the room until tomorrow morning, but he checked all the drawers. I assume he was making sure they were empty."

"Thanks for the information," Rodriguez said. "I'll let the other officers know." He frowned. "I wonder why they left the plants?"

"I think the plan was to get them later. One of the poachers went to pick up one of the bags and the handler shook his head."

"We're collecting fingerprints," Stanton said. "I'll be sure the team focuses on the drawers. I doubt we'll have any background on the Asians, but we might on the handler."

I straightened my back. "I might be able to help. The Silver Sentinels and the Succulent Saviors have done some scouting around the marina. They believe the men have been having the plants taken by boat to somewhere near San Francisco and loaded into a container."

Rodriguez nodded. "We've been thinking the same thing. We were aware of activity at the marina but haven't been able to get the evidence we need for a search warrant. Now we have it. The Coast Guard believes they know the tanker that will be used for both the plants and the men. I've notified the appropriate parties, search warrants are on the way, and I think we'll end this operation tonight."

"It would be nice to have that off our work list," Stanton said. "Along with the kidnappings. It still leaves us with Eric's murder and the wine theft."

I appreciated the fact he didn't refer to it as Phil's wine theft. It did, however, bring me back to what still needed to be resolved that had been put on hold with the immediacy of the kidnapping.

Phil's framing.

Eric's murder.

A vision of Phil's haggard face came into my mind.

The Silver Sentinels and I still had work ahead.

I hoped we could find the answers soon.

Chapter 17

"Do you need me for anything more, Deputy Stanton?" Michael asked.

"No, that will do it for now. I'm glad both you and the young lady are okay."

"Me too. Time for a nap, cleaning up, and getting ready for tonight's opening event."

Stanton shook his head. "You're going through with your plans?"

"You bet. It's not easy to gather a group like this together. I hope what they see and learn will change the lives of a lot of people."

"You're an amazing man, Michael. It's a privilege to know you."

The two clasped hands.

Scott and Michael started to walk off.

Scott turned. "Kelly, I'll call you so we can catch up."

"Okay," I replied.

"Good work finding Cassie earlier," Stanton said to me. "It was a relief to get one person off our search list." Stanton raised his eyebrows. "And, of course, rescuing Michael and Julie."

"Thanks." I knew he wasn't happy with me and appreciated what I felt was a peace offering.

"And your fliers were very well done," he added.

"I'm going to enjoy taking them down now that everyone is safe."

The deputy's phone rang. "Stanton here." He listened for a few minutes. "Okay. Call Davidson. He'll be dismantling the search and rescue set up. Tell him the situation and ask him to send some officers to look for them."

Warden Rodriguez and I looked at him questioningly.

"My men found the van where you said you left it. No one was there."

"The crash happened not far from the marina. Maybe they were able to get there and join their friends," I said.

Stanton nodded. "Possible."

The warden's phone went off with a text alert. He read what was there and informed us the warrants had arrived. "A team is assembling now. We'll raid the boats they've been using as soon as everyone is in place."

"Kelly," Stanton asked. "Do you have photos of the kidnappers?"

"Yes, they're on my camera. I can email them to you when I get back to my computer. I didn't get a good picture of the second man's face, but I saw it."

"I'd like to have the photos as well," Rodriguez said.

They gave me the email addresses they wanted me to use.

The warden looked at me. "Would you be willing to go to the marina and see if the men are among the ones we arrest?"

"Sure," I said.

Stanton stood. "I'll follow you. I'll let the officers inside know what's happening, and then I'll be right behind you."

I went to my Jeep. I got in but didn't see Rex's face in the rearview mirror. Concerned, I got out and opened the tailgate. He was curled up in a tight ball, not moving, not wagging his tail.

"I get it, Rex. You lost your mom, you found your mom, and then you lost your mom again. You'll be happy again shortly." I patted him and closed the hatch.

The drive to the marina didn't take long. As I approached it, I saw a number of California Department of Fish and Wildlife vehicles parked in a lot above the docks, out of sight of anyone below. The raid would be a surprise. Rodriguez hadn't told me not to go on down. I either needed to stay up here or go to the marina and be out of the way. I decided on the latter. I might see something that would be helpful to the officers.

I parked in the first available space that provided shade and rolled the windows down a bit. There were other spots closer to the docks, but I wanted to leave them open for the wardens. Vans similar to the ones I'd located a short while ago occupied much of the lot. As usual, the slight smell of fish permeated the air.

I decided to go to Joe's bait shop. His place was on the list for displaying fliers. I'd have the pleasure of taking the photos down and giving him the good news.

He was at his usual post with his thumbs hooked under the straps of his bib overalls. The bag with the binoculars hung on the arm of the rocking chair, and his baseball cap was shoved back on his gray curls. A camera now dangled next to the bag.

His face lit up when he saw me, and he rubbed his hands together. "All righty then, the fun is about to begin. My police magnet is here."

I shook my head and smiled. Joe was convinced I had some other-world connection to be able to attract the police. I'd given up trying to change his mind. The activities that were about to take place would only enforce his belief.

"Hey, Joe." I spotted the flier next to the doorway. "Good news." I took it down. "We've located all of our missing people, and they weren't hurt."

A big grin displayed his missing front tooth. "Hallelujah! So often situations involving missin' people don't end happily."

I nodded. "I know."

"Ivan and Rudy will be thrilled. They're on their boat. They were checkin' a couple of things on her and then comin' back to copy my surveillance data I've been gatherin' for the wardens. I was goin' to print my photos for them as well."

"Did you get a new camera?" I asked.

"Yep. Thought I might get some pictures to help the wardens."

No reason not to tell him. He'd know soon enough. "You won't need to do that. I know you like police drama with flashing lights and action. You're about to get some."

I filled him in on what was going to take place.

"Good. There's been a different feelin' about the men's actions. More of them around and seem to be movin' faster. Figured somethin' was about to give."

There was no cell phone service here, so it was unlikely the brothers knew about Cassie, Julie, and Michael being found alive.

"I'll go let Ivan and Rudy know about the people being found." I turned to go.

"Wait up a sec," Joe said.

When I turned back around, wrinkles had appeared on his face I hadn't noticed before. "The fellas said you and the Sentinels were tryin' to figure out who killed Eric. Nice young man. A real loss. He used to help me out summers and some weekends when he was in high school."

"Sorry, Joe," I said.

"I been by to pay my respects to his ma. She thanked me for the visit." He studied his hands, gnarled with arthritis. "His ma is all broken up. Lost her husband a while back. Luckily, her other two sons and her daughter are with her."

I'd known so little about Eric, this glimpse into his family life and the grief his death had brought made my stomach churn, and dealing with his death came slamming back into my life.

The Sentinels and I will do our best to find his killer.

"Thanks for letting me know. I'll talk with Phil Xanthis. He and Eric were friends. I'm sure he'll be willing to go see her."

"Appreciate it," Joe said.

I walked down the dock to the pride and joy of the Doblinsky brothers, the *Nadia*. They no longer took their fishing boat out, but they kept her in pristine shape. The metal railings gleamed and the sparkling white paint looked new and provided a sharp contrast for the boat's name written in bold, black letters on the bow.

Still no sign of the officers, but I was sure that would change shortly. I walked up the ramp and knocked on the door. I could see down into the cabin. Rudy appeared and waved me in.

I entered and descended the ladder. "No need to put up any more fliers. Everyone's been found and will soon be home safe and sound."

I had wondered at one point if I'd be able to say those words. They were music to my ears.

"Splendid," Rudy said.

"Yah," Ivan chimed in.

Part of the parking lot was visible through side windows. We didn't get any further about what happened because law enforcement cars were streaming in.

"There's about to be some action involving the poachers," I warned them.

The brothers joined me, saw the cars, and hurried to retrieve three sets of binoculars from a drawer.

Rudy handed me one. "We keep an extra pair for guests. No reason not to see what happens."

I put them up to my eyes and adjusted them. The officers were now running toward the dock. One of their vehicles parked at the far end blocked that gate. They ran past us and split up in teams, targeting three motorboats tied to the pier.

Sirens and flashing lights from the parking lot pulled my attention in that direction. A white van had tried to make a run for it but hadn't succeeded. I noticed a sheriff's car and figured that was Stanton. He must've decided to wait and come in with the others so as not to spook the poachers.

On the docks, men were being handcuffed. The officers began to lead them down the wooden pathway. Rudy, Ivan, and I went topside. Warden

Rodriguez wanted me to see if I recognized anyone. This seemed as good a way as any to find out.

Two boats up, an officer emerged with a man at gunpoint. The two turned in my direction, and I recognized the man in his green jacket and stained trousers as one of the kidnappers. The officer reached for a pair of handcuffs. At that moment, the poacher spun around and jumped into the water.

The officer fired a warning shot in the water near the man, but he didn't stop.

The amount of splashing the poacher was doing told me he wasn't a strong swimmer. He'd not gotten far from the dock when he began flailing his arms. I could see he was having trouble staying afloat. The heavy jacket, now waterlogged, would be dragging him down.

Rudy unlatched a life preserver and handed it to his bigger, stronger brother. Ivan tossed the doughnut into the water with a rope trailing behind it. It was a good throw, but it didn't reach the man. The swimmer's head disappeared from sight then bobbed back up again.

He sank down once more.

"He's drowning!" I shouted.

The officer who had fired the shot had dumped his coat on the dock and was unbuckling his heavy leather belt. Then I saw his sturdy lace up boots. He was far from being ready to go in the water.

I tore off my jacket and pulled off my shoes and socks. The water was calm, and I was a strong swimmer. The man's face appeared for an instant and then went under the water. Rudy offered me a life jacket.

"No time," I yelled.

I went to the railing, climbed over it, and jumped in. The shock of the cold water stunned me for an instant, then I surfaced and exhaled. I took in a deep breath, along with some drops of salt water. The ocean wasn't rough in the bay, but there were still currents and swells.

I began a head-high crawl toward the man, keeping him in sight as best I could as he momentarily appeared. Reaching the life preserver, I treaded water, picked it up, and tossed it in the direction of the poacher. Still not close enough. I swam to the doughnut and pushed it to within reach of the man, being careful not to get so close he could grab me. They had stressed in my water safety lessons that a panicked person could take you down with them. He clutched the preserver and crawled onto it enough to stay afloat.

I had a hold on the rope and felt it go taut. The poacher and I began to slowly move toward the *Nadia*. I worked my way down the rope to get farther away from the man and glanced at the boat. Ivan and Rudy were pulling. They were joined by one of the wardens.

We got to the side of the boat and then were pulled along to the stern and then around to the dock area. I let go, treaded water, and watched what was happening. The ocean current pushed the escapee into the rough wooden pilings. An officer held the life preserver line tightly and pulled him to where officers could reach him from the dock. Stanton and another man each grabbed an arm and tugged him onto the boards. They had successfully landed their fish.

"Kelly," Rudy yelled.

I looked up and saw a rope ladder dangling over the side. That would be better than hitting the wooden beams. The movement of the currents made it difficult to grab, and my cold hands had difficulty curling around the rough rope. Eventually, I managed to make a slow ascent. Warm hands grabbed me as I reached the railing and helped me over.

I shivered as a breeze hit my soaked clothes.

"Come. Downstairs now," Ivan said.

He put his arm around my shoulders. I was trembling uncontrollably.

"Let me go ahead to help you with the ladder," Rudy said.

He hurried to the cabin and disappeared into the boat. When I got there, I found him positioned near the bottom of the ladder. His hands steadied my legs as I inched my way down.

Once I was at the bottom, he wrapped a blanket around me. "Come here, next to the heater."

I pressed against the heater vents.

Stanton descended the ladder and joined us. "Are you okay?"

I nodded. "The one that tried to escape is one of the kidnappers."

"I figured as much," Stanton said. "What will happen to these men for poaching isn't enough to risk their life for. They'll get a fine, maybe some jail time. Kidnapping is another story."

Stanton left and Rudy put a hand on my shoulder. "I put one of my shirts and a pair of trousers in the bathroom for you to change into as well as towels."

I nodded. "Thanks."

My trembling had abated with the heat. I went into the ship's small bathroom and toweled off as best I could. I peeled off my clammy jeans and blouse. A few minutes with a hair dryer made my underwear go from soaking to damp. Livable.

Rudy's clothes worked surprisingly well, once I rolled up the pants bottoms and the shirtsleeves. I spent a few more minutes with the dryer on my hair. No fashion statement, just trying to get warm.

Rolling my wet clothes up, I carried them into the main cabin. Rudy handed me a clean plastic garbage bag, and I dropped them into it. Ivan gave me a steaming mug of lemon-scented tea. The hot liquid and the warmth of the mug made me feel almost normal again.

"Well, that was exciting." I inhaled the sweet-smelling steam from the hot liquid.

"Yah," Ivan said, "for all of us. Not do again, please."

He'd brought down my shoes, socks, and jacket. I put them on and felt real warmth returning to my feet.

A knock on the door announced the arrival of Warden Rodriguez. He came down the ladder and joined us. "How are you feeling?"

I smiled. "Almost back to normal."

"Stanton arrested the man you saved from drowning. Said you identified him as one of the kidnappers."

"That's correct."

"Do you feel up to looking at the other men to see if the second kidnapper is among them?"

"Yes, I can do that."

He handed me a camera. "We lined them up in the parking lot and photographed each of them."

Rodriguez showed me how to scroll through the photos.

I handed the camera back to him. "The other one's not there."

"We had an officer here as soon as we heard about the kidnappers being found and the connection to the poachers. While we waited for the warrant, he filmed a boat being loaded and leaving."

He gave me the camera once again and showed me how to watch a video on it.

"That's him." I paused the video and turned the camera so he could see what I'd just watched.

Whoever had filmed it had gotten a close-up. The man's pockmarked face and sparse beard clearly identified him.

Rodriguez nodded. "Thought it might be from your description. This works out well for us. The Coast Guard is following the boat to confirm the tanker that's being used to smuggle the plants and men out of the country. Having a kidnapper to arrest will give law enforcement much more clout."

I suddenly felt drained. My shoulders sagged, and I ran my fingers through my still-damp hair. "Do you need me for anything else?"

"No. I appreciate your help."

I bid Rodriguez and the brothers *adieu* and plodded down the dock. As I passed Joe's shop, I saw him behind the counter waiting on a customer.

Kidnappers caught.

Poachers caught.

A criminal who framed Phil still to go.

And a murderer.

Chapter 18

Stanton stood next to his patrol car, his soaked prisoner in the back. "I thought I'd wait and see if you identified the second guy,"

"I did." I relayed my conversation with Rodriguez.

"Good. I received a radio message that Julie's ready to be released and my men have finished taking a statement from her. Do you want to pick her up or have us drive her home? What's your preference?"

The tiredness vanished as the excitement of Julie being okay pushed it away.

"I'll go get her. Besides, that'll get her reunited with her dog more quickly." I decided to take Rex for a brief walk.

He was in his same forlorn position in the back. When we returned to the Jeep, I put his service dog vest on. He began to wag his tail. Working meant Julie.

I closed the hatch and made the short drive to the hospital. Julie was standing outside, her face uplifted to the sun. I imagined she was enjoying her freedom and the beautiful day. I got out, put a leash on Rex, and started walking in her direction. I could tell he wanted to bound ahead, but he was well-trained and the leash remained slack as he heeled beside me.

Julie began to turn toward me.

I unleashed the cattle dog but held onto his collar.

Julie saw me and then her dog. "Rex!" she shouted.

I released him, and he raced to her and danced on his hind legs.

She hugged him. "I'm so glad you're okay." A few tears trickled down her cheeks. Julie hugged him again.

"Let's get you back to the inn," I said.

"Sounds like a good idea to me."

I saw her do a double take when she noticed what I was wearing.

I laughed. "I had to borrow some clothes from a friend. I'll explain on our drive."

She got into the passenger seat and put on her seat belt. Rex immediately jumped in after her and planted himself on top of both of her feet. No back of the Jeep for him. She wouldn't be going anywhere without him any time soon.

I was more than fine with that.

Julie picked up one of the fliers resting on the seat between us. "Who created this?"

I started the car. "A group of crime-solving senior citizens called the Silver Sentinels, myself, and Scott Thompson...along with a gentleman who owns a print shop in Fort Peter."

"Thank you. I'd like to meet the group and thank them as well."

I pulled onto the highway. "I know they'd love to meet you."

"If you can get the name of the printer, I'll send him a thank you note," she added.

"I can do that."

She leaned back into the seat with a weary sigh. "Have you heard the story from Michael?"

I nodded.

"What he might not have told you is what happened with Rex. He didn't attack them, but he wouldn't leave my side. I explained to the one who spoke English he was my service dog. He was one of the kidnappers, but he had a heart. Said he had a cousin with a problem like mine. We walked to the car, and I ordered Rex inside."

"I'm so glad he wasn't hurt," I said.

"Me, too."

I glanced at her. "How are you feeling?"

"Tired and I don't remember much from the time when I had the seizure. That's normal when I have one."

"I found Cassie." I told her the story as we drove.

Julie sighed. "I ran into the poachers shortly after she left."

"She feels terrible," I said.

"I don't think it would've made any difference if she was there. They would've taken both of us. They were determined not to get caught. The poachers were so close to leaving the country, they weren't taking any chances."

I shared what had taken place while she was recovering from her seizure.

Julie leaned over and rubbed Rex's ears. "I'm glad most of the poachers were arrested and the nightmare's over. I'm sure the police will get the rest of them."

"I believe they will as well."

We reached the inn and I spotted Cassie's car in the lot. Next to it was a white Chevrolet pickup.

Julie got out, along with Rex, and, at the same time, Cassie emerged from her car and ran to us, wrapping Julie in her arms. "I'm so, so sorry. It's my fault." The tears streamed down her face.

Julie hugged her in return. "Cassie, it would've happened even if you had been there. It's okay. It all worked out."

While they'd been talking, Sebastian had gotten out of the other vehicle. He stood a few feet away. It didn't look like his tousled blond hair had been brushed today.

Julie saw him. "Sebastian, hi!" She gave him a rueful smile. "Sorry to miss our cooking session yesterday. I would much rather have been with you than where I was."

"I wish you would've been here with me as well...I'm so glad you're okay...I was so worried." He glanced at Cassie. "They announced you'd been found at the search and rescue command post. Your friend and I immediately came here to wait for you."

Cassie nodded. "They didn't give us any particulars, other than you were okay, so we took a leap of faith you'd come back here today."

Sebastian held up the stainless-steel tool, the implement he'd shown me yesterday. "Uh...I got you this. I was going to give it to you yesterday as a thank you for helping me so much."

He handed her the metal oval with the different-sized holes and the slit resembling an open mouth.

She turned it around and examined it from different angles. "What is it?"

"It's a kale and herb scraper. I remember you said chefs were always looking for new ways to save time."

"Awesome. We'll have to experiment using it together."

"Uh...I know you probably don't feel like cooking tomorrow afternoon, but I thought I'd ask," Sebastian said.

"Getting back to normal, which for me is cooking, would be the best medicine."

Sebastian's eyes widened. "Really? You want to get together tomorrow afternoon?"

"You bet."

"I'm so glad to hear that." He took a step toward her then stopped. "I'll see you then."

I wondered if he'd been thinking of hugging her but then decided he didn't know her well enough. I'd seen the look on his face and heard the anxiety in his voice when she was missing and knew he had feelings for her.

Julie settled his indecision by walking to him and giving him a quick hug. "Thanks for the present. I'm looking forward to us cooking together tomorrow."

"Tomorrow then." Sebastian turned to leave, his cheeks flushed, grinning from ear to ear.

I had picked up the fliers as I'd followed Julie out of the Jeep and now I held them up. "I'm thrilled to say we can toss these in the recycling bin now. Would you like to do the honors?" I asked her.

"Very much so. I want to save one to remind myself that every day is a gift," Julie said.

Cassie held out her hand. "I'd like one, too, for the same reason."

I handed each of them one and the three of us walked up the back steps. A blue bin with a recycling symbol rested in the corner. I lifted the lid and Julie threw the fliers in with a flourish.

"Do you want me to see if the Silver Sentinels are here so you can thank them, or do you want to wait until another time?"

Julie was silent for a moment. Then looking at the flier she held, she said, "I'd like to do it now. You never know what the next day might bring." Julie turned to Cassie. "These are the people, along with Kelly and Scott Thompson, who are responsible for creating and distributing the fliers."

We entered and Helen, who was standing at the counter, turned and exclaimed, "Julie, I heard you'd been found! I'm so glad you're okay."

She gave Julie a big hug.

Hugging was the theme for the day and for good reason.

"Are the Sentinels here?" I asked.

Helen nodded. "I just refreshed their coffee."

"Follow me," I said.

Cassie tagged along behind Julie. Rex stayed glued to Julie's side.

I opened the door to the conference room and entered, along with the two women. The five seniors who comprised the group rushed forward and another round of hugs ensued, along with profuse words of thanks from Julie and Cassie. I made the introductions.

"I know we haven't met," Mary said, "but I feel like I know both of you after seeing your faces on the flyers."

"Kelly came up with the idea." Gertie said.

Julie turned to me. "You didn't tell me it was your brainchild."

Warmth filled my face, indicating one of my blushes had started. "We all worked together. Speaking of which, Professor, Julie would like the name and address of the printer who helped."

"Of course, my dear." He sat and began writing on a piece of notepaper.

"I'd like the information as well," Cassie said.

The Professor nodded and tore off a second sheet.

"Thank you again, everyone," Julie said.

Cassie nodded. "Yes. Thank you for caring about us."

The Professor handed each of them a slip of paper. "It's been a pleasure to meet you both."

The women left, and I poured myself a cup of coffee, taking a moment to enjoy the fragrance of the strong, dark roast. I plopped into a chair.

A quiet knock on the door was followed by Phil's face peeking in. "I saw your Jeep and decided to find out what happened."

"Have a seat," I said. "We're just beginning to get caught up."

Mary handed me a plate with a chocolate brownie studded with chunks of chocolate. Coffee and chocolate, my two favorites. I might recover after all.

"Rudy and Ivan filled us in on what happened at the marina," Mary said.

The Professor nodded. "Quite the daring feat, my dear."

I shrugged. "I was glad I had the necessary training. My mother insisted all of us kids not only know how to swim well, but how to handle emergencies. We spent a lot of time on high mountain lakes in the summer. The lifeguard approach stroke I used today was part of what I was taught."

Rudy leaned over toward Phil and whispered, "I'll tell you about this later."

Phil nodded.

"Still very brave," Gertie said. "Now, how about the rest of the story? How did the kidnappers get found and Michael and Julie freed?"

"And Cassie," Mary chimed in. "What was she doing?"

I told the story. They did the punctuation with oohs and aahs. By the time I ate a second brownie, they were up to date.

"Time to regroup and plan our next steps," Mary said.

"I agree," the Professor said. "With the wardens' successful raid at the marina, I feel we can officially take the poachers off our investigation list."

Gertie nodded. "We still have Eric's death and Phil's situation to resolve."

My phone alerted me to a text. Warden Rodriguez's message said they hadn't found the handler on the tanker and asked if there were any photos of him.

"The next thing to do just got delivered." I relayed the message to the Sentinels.

"I'll check with Rupert," Gertie said. "However, finding the handler is up to the police, at this point. He could be anywhere in the country. I agree with you we are done with the poachers."

We all nodded in agreement.

Gertie continued, "Other than contacting Rupert, I feel we need to put our investigations aside until after Saturday's event. We owe it to Michael, for all he's done for us and the community." She looked at Phil. "I hope you understand, Phil."

"Absolutely," he said. "I'm in tremendous debt to him. I'm not going anywhere soon. There's time to figure out my predicament."

"Michael is going on with the party tonight. Are any of you going?" I asked.

"We heard the opening reception was still on and discussed attending," the Professor said, "but we decided not to. We are all doing presentations tomorrow and want to prepare for those."

"We dropped everything to get the fliers out," Mary said. "We're going to work together this evening to polish what we plan to say."

I'd noticed Phil's eyes widen until he had a deer-in-the-headlights look about him.

"Phil, are you okay?"

"Uh…did I hear you say Michael is having his event tonight? The one with the wine and cheese?"

I nodded.

"The one Andy and I planned what seems like eons ago? The one where I'm pouring wine and he's serving cheese?"

I nodded again.

"Egads." He ran his hand over his unshaven face. "It completely dropped out of my mind with all that's happened."

It didn't surprise me Scott hadn't checked with him. I suspected that had dropped out of his mind as well.

Phil jumped up, almost knocking over his chair. "I've got to get ready. Luckily, I dropped the wine off there earlier this week. I'll call Andy." He left as he chose a number on his phone.

"I'll keep the war room operating as long as I can," I said. "There are no meetings scheduled for a while." I turned to Rudy. "I'll get your clothes back to you tomorrow."

"No hurry," he replied.

"Are you going tonight?" Ivan asked me.

"To be honest, I hadn't thought about it, either. Michael wanted as many managers to attend as possible so we could help answer questions. If he can do it, so can I." I stood.

We said our goodbyes, and I walked to my quarters. I'd have to put on some speed to get ready in time for the evening party. I emailed the photos I had of the kidnappers to Stanton and Rodriguez. Since they had the bearded one on video and knew where he was, it wasn't critical. However, it might be useful in some way.

My phone rang as I sent the second message.

"Hello, Scott," I said after seeing his name in caller ID.

"Hi," he replied. "Well, Michael is sleeping and the money is headed back to San Francisco. I thought this might be a good time to hear the rest of Michael's story. Michael and I spent the ride back talking about the organization of tonight's event."

He didn't know about my ocean swim.

"Actually, it's not a great time. I'll be at the center tonight and will fill you in then. Does that work?"

"Sure. I didn't know if you were coming or not. I'm glad to hear you plan to be there. See you tonight."

I wondered what his reaction would be when he found out I'd jumped in the water to save a drowning kidnapper…and then there was the murder investigation we were still involved in.

Chapter 19

While getting ready for the evening get together, I scanned the schedule for Michael's party. He'd stressed casual attire and encouraged people to adopt a western theme throughout their stay. Saturday, the day of the cooking event, guests and participants were invited to come in costume. Tonight's reception started at five thirty and would only last an hour and a half. Cheese, wine, and light appetizers would be served.

I remembered him saying he wanted people to have an opportunity to dine out and enjoy the area's fine restaurants. Guests could sign up in advance for a light box dinner if they wanted to stay in for the evening. Friday, he'd provide a full lunch and dinner and, Saturday, the chefs would offer their special dishes. People would stroll from one booth to the next and have an opportunity to sample all the creations.

Tomorrow morning, various groups would make presentations. The Silver Sentinels would address what the center had done for the community and some of their friends. The veterans would describe what impact it had on their lives and do a PTSD service dog training demonstration. Others would talk about the classes being offered.

In the afternoon, tours of the center would be given, as well as mini-classes, including goat yoga. Remembering my earlier encounters with the goats, I was sure this would prove entertaining. Michael wanted people to mingle and talk on a personal basis, so the afternoon would also provide a chance for guests and presenters to visit. Optional winery tours were offered in the afternoon on both days.

I put on a clean pair of jeans and pulled my riding boots out of the closet. I put on a white blouse with a hint of a western design on the back

and added a tooled leather belt. I'd save the silver buckle I'd won barrel
racing for Saturday.

Costumes for some people, everyday attire for me on the ranch back
home. I'd brought some of my western wear and riding equipment to
Redwood Cove. I'd been able to ride Nezi, an appaloosa at the nearby
Redwood Cove Ranch, and hoped to do more.

When I arrived at the community center, veterans were acting as valets
to park cars in the main lot near the barn. I spied a Ferrari that looked like
the one that had been at the inn. There were other exotic cars, but plenty
of the vehicles didn't shout money.

Deciding not to bother the valets, I parked over by the lounge area. It
would make for a longer walk, but I didn't mind. I enjoyed the fresh air
tinged with the scent of the redwoods. If the llamas were out, I could visit
with them. It would be dark when I returned, so I got the small flashlight
out of the glove box and slipped it into my purse.

I made it to the barn, not having seen any llamas but feeling refreshed.
I paused for a moment and looked at the courtyard area where the Search
and Rescue task force had been set up. No trace of it remained.

Julie and Michael had been missing for only about twenty-four hours.
What a long period of time it had seemed. I knew now what people meant
when they said time seemed to stand still. I took a deep breath and went in.

The barn looked like one instead of a state-of-the-art meeting facility.
Bales of hay were scattered about, providing informal seating areas. Benches
had been brought in and covered with soft blankets. Their colorful designs
reminded me of Native American saddle blankets. Saddles mounted on
sawhorses were here and there, with bridles over the saddle horns. The
back doors were open and the flames of an outside campfire could be seen
dancing in the darkening night.

Garl strolled into the room with his massive harlequin Great Dane, Toby,
on his right side. At his left side was none other than the miniature black
and white goat Sparky. He had been placed on a swivel lead, allowing
him to run in circles.

Garl settled on a bale of hay and his dog lay down at his feet. Sparky
jumped on the dog's back, slid down his shoulder, and sat on Toby's curled
up front legs. Guests pointed, laughed, and headed toward them.

A crowd assembled around Garl and the animals. People asked if it
was okay to pet them.

"Sure. Be careful, though," Garl added as an open-mouthed Sparky
headed for a diamond dangling from a gold chain as a woman bent to pet

him. Garl was quicker and grabbed him back in time. "The little guy will eat anything, or at least try to get a taste."

A woman with long hair pulled back just as Sparky decided maybe it was brown hay and worth a bite.

The farm manager, Jim Patterson, entered leading Annie, the curly-haired reddish-brown llama I'd named after Orphan Annie. When the center's herd of llamas had arrived, Scott had let the Silver Sentinels and me name them. Each of the Sentinels had their "own" llama.

I went over to him. "Hi, Jim. Thanks for bringing my llama."

"My pleasure," he replied.

I ran my fingers through the llama's soft hair. She gazed at me with those beautiful, huge brown eyes and batted her long lashes.

I held out my hand to show her it was empty. "Sorry. I didn't know you were going to be here, or I would have brought you a treat."

She brushed her soft lips against my palm as if to say she understood.

"I'll make it up to you tomorrow." I gave her a last pat and then wandered over to where Phil and Andy were working. "You made it."

Phil rolled his eyes. "I didn't think I could move so fast."

It was nice to see him so animated after what he'd been through the last few days.

Andy offered me a plate with several slices of cheese and some crackers. "I was a little ahead of Phil. I didn't know if the event would go on or not, so I prepared myself just in case." He glanced at his friend. "I haven't had the worries to deal with that Phil has had."

Phil handed me a glass of white wine. "This Sagatini sauvignon blanc will go well with those cheeses."

Andy pointed to the first slice. "That's Blue Castello from Denmark. You'll find it creamy with a buttery taste." He went on to describe the other two cheeses.

I put one of the slices on a cracker. "Thanks."

I took a bite and followed it with a sip of wine. Phil was right. The cold beverage was semi-dry, with a hint of sweetness, and paired well with the cheese.

"I'll see you later," I said. "I promised Scott I'd bring him up to date."

Before I could find Scott, I spied Michael conversing with several guests. He appeared relaxed and refreshed and didn't have a hair out of place. Nothing to indicate he'd spent the night on a cot in a motel room surrounded by kidnappers. Resilient, to say the least.

Veterans in western wear circulated throughout the room with trays of light snacks.

One of them, a young woman, approached and held out her offerings. "Would you like a mushroom tart?"

A pang of hunger reminded me I'd had half of a sandwich for lunch. I took one and thanked her. As I wandered, I passed a table off in a corner of the room with several large ice chests on it. A list of names had been taped on the side of each. I guessed these were the box dinners people had requested in advance.

"Hello, everyone." Michael held a microphone and stood in the middle of the room.

I checked my watch and saw it was five forty-five.

"I want to welcome you and thank you all for coming. This evening's event is meant to give you an opportunity to mingle and get to know each other. I know some of you are friends already. Gift bags are on the table at the entrance. The schedules for Friday and Saturday are in there, along with a few other items. You're welcome to take your bag and look through it now. If you have any questions, please don't hesitate to ask me. That's all. Enjoy the evening."

As Michael began to mingle and converse, Lorenzo entered the building, saw me, and came over. "I understand you were involved in finding the missing people. Congratulations."

The small-town rapid-fire communication systems were still functioning.

"Thanks." I'd told the story enough and still had another rehash of it to go with Scott. I wasn't going to get into it now. It would be in the news soon enough, especially because of Michael's involvement.

"Any more news about Phil?" Lorenzo asked.

Remembering his earlier assumption that Phil was guilty, I looked him in the eye and smiled. "No, but since he's innocent, it'll be over soon." I raised the glass. "I'm really enjoying your sauvignon blanc. Your family does an excellent job."

He blinked a couple of times then went along with my change of subject. "Thank you. We've made our name, won our share of awards. We've enjoyed the business, but my father wants to retire, and I want to try something new."

I could understand his desire as I'd experienced it myself with my decision to leave my parents' ranch.

He continued, "We're keeping the family home and a fair amount of acreage, mostly with vines. We can sell the grapes and not have to be involved in the actual wine-making process. I'll be building a home on part of the land. We're selling the business end of wine making, like the cellars, equipment, tasting room, etcetera."

I detected no hint of the upset I'd unintentionally overheard between him and his father. "What are you planning to do?"

The next few minutes were filled with details of his real estate adventure. There was no missing the excitement in his voice. I believed loving what you did for a living was so important, and it sounded like he thought he'd found his place.

"I wish you the best," I said.

"Thanks." He gave a final nod and went on his beaming way.

I turned at a light touch on my arm and found myself staring into Scott's blue eyes.

"Glad you decided to come." He glanced around the room. "Everyone appears to be in animated conversation with each other or one of the resort's managers. Let's take a few minutes and you can fill me in on the rest of Michael's story."

I could see the flames of the campfire out back. "Sure." I might as well get it over with. "Let's go enjoy the fire."

"Okay," he said.

I managed to snag a few more appetizers on the way. A sign posted next to the open back doors read "S'mores this way."

"S'mores! I haven't had those in years," I exclaimed. "Let's make some."

Scott frowned. "What are those?"

I paused and looked at him. "Really? You don't know what s'mores are? You never had any when you went camping as a child?"

"We never went camping. It was big city to big city, boarding school to boarding school."

Oh, my. And he was a gourmet cook. It'd be interesting to see where this led.

"Well, here's how it works," I said.

A table held graham crackers, milk chocolate bars, and marshmallows. A row of roasting sticks leaned against the table. Someone had whittled them into the perfect size and shape. Michael was going for authentic experiences.

I got two plates and put two squares of graham crackers on each of them. I placed a piece of the milk chocolate on two of them, enough to cover the cracker. I put a couple of marshmallows on a stick and handed it to him.

Now thoroughly bewildered, he asked, "Now what?"

"Be patient. I'll show you."

I prepared a stick for myself. "Now you toast the marshmallows. The trick is to brown and not burn them and to get them away from the fire before they are so gooey they fall off. When they're done, you put them on the chocolate."

Folding chairs had been placed around the fire. I pulled a couple close enough for us to sit as we toasted our marshmallows.

A cooking challenge. Scott could handle this. I didn't think a couple of marshmallows over an open fire had ever received the kind of attention they got as Scott toasted his.

He pulled them out just as they began to sag and scraped them onto his chocolate-covered cracker. Mine were right behind his.

"Now you take the remaining cracker and put it on top. You're making a sandwich of sorts." I demonstrated. "Then you eat them."

The intense sweetness thrilled my taste buds. I'd forgotten how good the simple combination tasted.

Scott did as instructed and took a bite. From the wide smile on his face, I could tell this simple campfire recipe had pleased him.

"You grew up on these?" he asked with one of his delightful impish grins. "No wonder you're so sweet."

I was glad it was too dark for him to see me blush. "It's standard fare for campers."

He took another bite. "Well, I'm in." He began to prepare another s'more. "Now tell me the rest of Michael's story and whatever else happened this afternoon, if anything."

If anything.

I hoped the s'more would keep him smiling as I told him about my watery escapade.

Chapter 20

As I started to tell Scott the part of Michael's story he'd missed, he picked up two more marshmallows and put them on his stick. He toasted them with the precision of a scientist, striving for a perfect even golden brown on all sides. Scott placed them on the cracker and chocolate he'd prepared and put the top on as I wound up my story.

"Thanks for sharing that." He took a bite. "And for teaching me how to make s'mores."

I considered making another one but remembered the times I'd overdone it as a kid and had gotten sick.

He finished his treat and wiped his hands on a napkin. "Kelly, I've always felt I understood why you and the Sentinels do what you do in terms of helping people, but I realize now it was only on an intellectual level. Now I know inside what it means to be an emotional recipient of the group's support. I never felt alone during the kidnapping ordeal."

"I'm glad to hear that. I know the Sentinels will be happy about it as well."

"It was a dark time for me, and all of you helped me through it. You won't hear me ever try to dissuade any of you from helping others," Scott said.

I wondered if this would apply to saving the drowning kidnapper. For a split second, I considered not saying anything regarding the incident but immediately rejected the thought. He'd asked about the rest of the afternoon. Omitting was a form of lying, and I wouldn't go there.

"What's next for you and the group?" he asked.

Putting it off, however, was fair.

"We're still trying to help Phil with the wine theft and find out who murdered Eric. Did you have a chance to see the charts referring to them when you were there?"

He shook his head. "I was too worried about Michael to notice anything."

I filled him in on what had happened and what we knew.

"Right now, the Sentinels want to do their best to support this event. After it's over, we'll have a meeting and dig in. Would you like to join us? You've seen how it works. We all brainstorm and figure out a plan. The more minds at work, the more likely we'll figure something out."

"I'd like to attend. Any way I can give back is important to me."

"I'll let you know when the next meeting is." I shook my head. "It's hard to believe it was only yesterday morning Phil was arrested. Everything around Phil and Eric ground to a halt when the search and rescue bell sounded."

The fire crackled and sparks flew in the air, dying before they came close to us.

Scott leaned back. "So, you grew up with campfires like this?"

"Oh, yeah. I've made many of them myself. We did overnight trips with our guests in the summer."

"Like sleeping out in the open? Did you have a tent?"

I laughed at the incredulous tone in his voice. "It varied. Most of the time we stayed at camps we'd created over the years. They had cabins or tents and corrals for the horses."

"You said most of the time…that means not all."

"Correct. We did a few trips each year where we slept out in the open in sleeping bags. Just like in the Old West. We tied up the horses and brought the dogs with us to guard them."

"Let me get this straight. You slept on the ground, with only the starry night sky for a roof."

"Correct again."

He shook his head. "Michael summed it up when he called you a Wyoming cowgirl."

"I think I just heard my name spoken," Michael said as he joined us.

Scott laughed. "You did. I was commenting on how aptly you described Kelly this afternoon."

"No lie. I made a good choice when I hired her."

Scott eagerly reached for his roasting stick. "Kelly taught me how to make s'mores. Would you like one?"

"Maybe later. I'm in the middle of a glass of fine cabernet in the barn. Using it to wash down chocolate, graham crackers, and marshmallow would be a crime."

"Let me know when," Scott said. "I was about ready to head back in to talk to the guests, but I can come out here and make you one any time."

Chapter 15

Scott didn't know about Ned Blaine. He wasn't a local, so the infamous smoking telephone lines wouldn't have included him. The newspaper only came out once a week on Tuesday, and that was before Ned was murdered.

"Kelly?"

"Someone shot and killed a reporter by the name of Ned Blaine. Daniel Stevens is a suspect. The man was found dead on sacred tribal land and notes he made indicate Daniel threatened him."

Scott stared. "Did Daniel do that?"

"He did, but he didn't threaten to kill him. The reporter questioned Allie and frightened her when he grabbed her arm. Daniel told him to never talk to her or touch her again."

Scott gave a weary sigh. "I know you and the Silver Sentinels do what you feel is necessary to help your friends and the community. I understand why you're looking into this, what with Daniel involved. I won't try to talk you and the others out of it, but I do worry about all of you. Like before, if there's something I can do to help, let me know."

"Thanks for understanding."

Scott put his hands on my shoulders. "Kelly, be careful. Promise me that."

"I promise."

The phone rang and Scott answered it. "Hello." He nodded a few times. "I can come over and help." He hung up.

I slipped on my coat and picked up my purse.

"A couple of the guys need my help moving some furniture. It shouldn't take more than about ten or fifteen minutes. Please let the Sentinels know I'll be a little late."

"Sure…and thank you again for a wonderful dinner."

"Let me walk you to the door so I can turn the lights on."

It had gotten dark while we cleaned up after dinner. Scott flipped a switch, and light flooded the yard.

"See you in a bit," I said.

"Sounds good."

I walked to my truck and got in. Scott closed the door.

I hadn't been to the Professor's house before, but his directions were impeccable, and I had no trouble finding it. A bright light shining on the brass house number confirmed it was the correct place. The house was painted dark gray with light gray trim and railings.

I parked and walked up a cement walkway bordered on both sides by a neatly trimmed lawn. A border of delicate yellow flowers lined the front of the house and lent a light perfume to the air. Wide steps led to a covered porch. I used a metal door knocker in the shape of an open book to announce my arrival.

The Professor opened the door. "My dear, I see you found us. Please come in."

I stepped in and warm air enveloped me, carrying a pleasant mixture of smoke laced with a hint of sweetness. A vase with the same blossoms I'd seen on the way in sat on a table next to a comfortably worn brown leather couch. A crackling fire burned in a wide stone fireplace, its flames dancing behind a screen.

A brown leather chair matching the couch angled in the fire's direction, a yellow and brown plaid blanket folded over one arm. Soft indentations mimicked the form of the most recent occupant. An oriental rug with a predominately orange and cream pattern covered a dark wood floor.

And books.

Books were everywhere.

Full bookshelves lined both sides of the fireplace and there were no empty spaces I could see. The coffee table had a stack, and the end table holding the flowers revealed a paperback with a protruding bookmark in the soft glow of a reading lamp. The far side of the room housed a floor-to-ceiling built-in bookcase and more books.

To my right was a brightly lit dining room. A chorus of hellos greeted me from the silver-haired Sentinels sitting around a table. The Professor hung my jacket in a coat closet, and we joined them.

"Would you like something to drink?" The Professor indicated a sideboard with coffee, tea, and water.

"Coffee would be nice. Thanks."

"No need to come back. Everything is going fine and there are plenty of people the attendees can talk to if they have questions." He held out two boxes. "Two of the guests won't arrive until late tonight. Their plane was delayed. I thought you two might like their dinners."

The word dinner made me realize how hungry I was. "I'd love one. It'll keep me from embarrassing myself by following the appetizer trays around the room."

He handed us each one and left. I opened the box and found a colorful salad with a multitude of vegetables including corn, beets, and green beans layered on fresh lettuce leaves. Strips of tender seasoned chicken crisscrossed the top. Two herb rolls occupied the corners of the box. Perfect.

We ate in silence for a few minutes. I had a feeling Scott was as famished as I was.

I decided this was a good time to tell Scott about my dive in the ocean. Good food and the distraction of eating might help.

I took a deep breath, opened my mouth, and said, "Scott—"

Before I could continue, Michael came out again. "I just got an update from Stanton. Thought you'd like to know. They haven't caught the handler yet, but the prints they found gave them his name, Andrew Winslow. He has quite a record." He chuckled and looked at me. "He also filled me in on the rest of the afternoon."

I rushed in and said, "That's what I was about to tell Scott."

"You've had quite a day. Let's see if I've got this straight. You found then rescued Julie and me, saved a drowning man, and taught the gourmet cook Scott Thompson how to make s'mores. Quite a full, diverse day." He turned to go. "Talk to you two later."

Scott put his fork down. "Drowning man?"

"I was just about to get to that."

I told him everything. He went back to his salad as he listened, albeit eating more slowly. My heart beat faster as I got to the part about jumping in to save the kidnapper and keeping my distance so he couldn't drag me down.

When I finished, Scott shook his head. "You're going to turn my hair gray sooner than later. Before you know it, I'll qualify to be a Silver Sentinel." He continued working on his salad.

That was it. No frowns. No words of caution.

Puzzled, I picked up a forkful of salad and began to eat.

Scott closed the lid of his box. "That hit the spot. I'm sorry the guests had their plane delayed, but I sure enjoyed their dinner."

He picked up his roasting stick. "Now, for dessert. One more. The others were appetizers."

Scott began cooking his marshmallows. "I've been thinking, Kelly. What I know about you from the past, today's events, and what I heard about your upbringing, I realized I've never met anyone like you. Not even close."

I didn't know if this was good or bad.

"I think that's why I've worried so much about you. It's hard for me to imagine someone doing the things you've done and not getting hurt." He pulled his perfect marshmallows away from the flames. "I've come to a decision. I'm at peace with who you are, how you act, and the risks you take. It's you. You're as careful as you can be. I know that. I'm not saying I won't worry, but…I'm at peace."

A shiver went through me. My ex-husband had never stopped trying to change me. He gave up and took up with my best friend instead.

"Thank you, Scott. I appreciate it. What you said means a lot to me."

Trust, together with honesty, and letting me be myself were my top three criteria for a relationship. I'd experienced the first with Scott in the past and now heard the second one from him. I had a sharp intake of breath and my heart beat a little faster…only this time not from fear. I wondered if Scott and I—

My thoughts were interrupted by a server offering us appetizers.

"No, thanks," I said.

The dinner had done the trick.

Scott declined as well. "Let's go back inside and see if we can be of any assistance. I'm refueled and ready to go."

He took my box and threw both into the recycling bin as we rejoined the party.

I'd get back to my thoughts later.

Sparky was the life of the party…literally. He was running in circles, bucking, leaping, twirling, and twisting. Dancing like only a goat could do. Garl had the end of Sparky's lead; otherwise, I'm sure he would've jumped on the wine and cheese table and tap danced his way through the bottles and trays. Toby remained sprawled in the position he'd assumed when he came in.

Phil began singing using "tas" and "das" punctuated by whistling, and he started to dance. He was doing an admirable rendition of "Zorba the Greek." Almost everyone in the room watched and clapped in time with the song. Scott and I joined in with the clapping. Suddenly, Phil grabbed my hand and pulled me behind him. He loved line dancing and knew I did as well. Soon a number of guests had joined us and we wound our way through the room. Phil finally stopped singing after a final "ta da."

The dancers all laughed. I heard comments about not having so much fun in years and what a fantastic event this was.

I hadn't noticed several large, heavyset men in various corners of the room when I had come in. They stood in the background, in the shadows as much as possible. One took a sip from a small bottle of Pellegrino. Probably the bodyguards. I went to the back door and looked out. Two veterans stood on the fringe of the barn's outside light. Michael had said there would be patrols as well.

The kind of carefree moments the guests had had with Sparky and Phil might not come often. Who knew money could carry such a burden? I wondered if any of them had received recent threats.

I hoped not for their sake, as well as the local police, who had a lot on their plate. There was still Phil's situation to resolve and Eric's murder. The Succulent Saviors said poachers had been arrested near where his body was found. Had one of them or the handler, Andrew Winslow, killed him?

Even though Julie and Michael said they'd been treated well, if Eric threatened the poachers' opportunity to be monetarily covered for the rest of their lives as the handler had said, that gave a strong motive to silence him. Maybe we'd find out once Winslow was arrested.

Life in prison would give him a strong motive to talk if someone else was to blame for Eric's death.

Chapter 21

The crowds began to thin. I spied Scott nearby in what appeared to be earnest conversation with a short man in tan slacks and a black jacket. The woman accompanying him wore an intricately embroidered denim shirt. Flowers swirled over the shoulder and down the right side of the garment. Her black leggings ended above sandals sprinkled with gold stars. A strand of diamonds hung from each of her ears, long enough to almost touch her shoulders.

Not wanting to interrupt, I texted Scott goodbye and let him know how much fun I'd had talking to him and that I'd be at the center in the morning. The barn area and parking lot were well lit. As I left the light behind and headed to the darkened area where I'd parked, I pulled my flashlight from my purse and switched it on. Walking to the Jeep, the events of the day caught up with me and I dragged myself up into the driver's seat and wearily closed the door. I put the flashlight back in the glove box. Sleep wouldn't be a problem tonight.

* * * *

The next morning, I went out the back door with Phil's breakfast. Julie and Rex were strolling in the gravel parking lot.

I stopped next to Julie. "Hi! Did you get a good night's sleep?"

A shadow passed over her face. "Pretty good. I think it will be a while before the kidnapping is behind me."

I could only imagine.

"I didn't thank you yesterday for taking care of Rex," Julie said. "Sorry. I really appreciate what you did for him."

"No problem. I was happy to help. You had a lot on your mind yesterday." I tilted my head to the side and smiled. "Are you going foraging this morning?"

She laughed. "No more of that for me. Ever. Sebastian said he'd go out and hunt for the wild edibles we need for the chili."

"Are you planning to listen to the presentations at the community center?"

She shook her head. "I'm going to rest, check out some more of your fantastic cookbooks in my room, and then get my ingredients and equipment together so I'm ready to start right after the other chefs leave."

"I'm looking forward to sampling what you two create."

Julie smiled. "Thanks, Kelly." She turned and started toward the inn. "See you later."

I climbed the steps to Phil's room. Just as I was about to set the basket down outside, the door opened.

"Good morning, Kelly." A clean-shaven Phil wore black slacks, a crisp white shirt, and one of his embroidered wine vests. A good sign. "Can you come in for a few minutes?"

"Sure. Your breakfast is my last delivery." I followed him in and set the basket on the table in the dining area.

Phil gazed at me seriously. "I want to thank you and the others for believing in me. It helps a lot. Please convey my message to the Sentinels." He picked up a mug of coffee from the counter in the kitchen area and took a sip. "I've decided to continue my work as usual...or at least as best I can. I'll need a different vehicle for wine deliveries, but today I only have consultation appointments, so the car will be fine. Tomorrow I'll be doing the two wine tasting classes for Michael's event."

I knew he'd visited a number of his customers to distribute the missing people photos. "Did anyone say anything to you about the thefts when you were passing out fliers?"

He shook his head. "A few whispers here and there and a furtive look or two."

"Have you heard anything from the private investigators?"

"They'll be able to inspect the van later today. They've made as detailed an analysis of what the thief looks like as they can, given the poor quality of the video."

"Hopefully they'll find evidence the car was tampered with in some way to make it start." I paused. "On another note, I talked to Joe at the marina. He knew Eric and said he went and visited his mother. It seemed to help her. Would you be willing to go see her?"

"Of course," he replied. "I know his mother and should have thought of that sooner myself."

"Well, you've been having a challenging time."

"True, so true." He sat at one of the chairs next to the table. "Eric lived at home, and I met him there a few times. On one occasion, I had dinner with them. I'll call her and set up a time."

"Another issue you were dealing with was the question as to whether your tasting is off in some way. Have you found out anything about that?"

"I double-checked my medications and didn't find any evidence they'd have a negative interaction with my taste buds. I couldn't think of any food or drink I received as a gift. I made a doctor's appointment for next week when I get home. I'll see what he has to say."

"It sounds like you've done everything you can for now. I'm glad you've decided to get back on track with your business," I said.

"Me, too." He looked at his watch. "On that note, I'd better get going."

"What about your breakfast?"

Phil reached into the basket. "I'll take it with me and eat between stops."

"Take the basket. I can get it from you later."

"Okay." He picked it up.

I trotted down the steps, happy about Phil feeling comfortable enough to go back to work. Right then, a deputy sheriff's car pulled in and parked next to my Jeep. Stanton got out. Maybe I'd gotten upbeat a little too soon. I frowned as I approached.

He waited next to the back porch for me. As I got near him, he said, "No need for the suspicious look. I'm not here with any bad news. Just stopping by for a cup of coffee and a chance to talk to Tommy about his new assignment."

My brow cleared. I'd better not plan on playing poker any time soon with my face so easy to read.

We entered the inn together. Tommy sat in his usual place at the counter, eating his breakfast. Fred sprawled nearby. Helen poured coffee into a mug and handed it to the deputy. She knew from previous visits he liked it black.

"Hi, Deputy Stanton," Tommy said.

Fred thumped the floor with his tail but didn't bother to get up.

Stanton put his mug on the counter. "Do you have any special plans for your three-day weekend, Tommy?"

"Mom and I are going to shop for supplies for my school project," he replied.

Helen smiled. "We'll go up to Fort Peter and then have lunch at the Creamery."

"Their sundaes are so good." Tommy slid off his stool. "I'll go get the directions for my assignment."

Helen looked questioningly at Stanton. "Are you sure you don't have time for breakfast?"

"No. Like I said in my text, I can only stay a short while. Lots of meetings." He looked at me. "I imagine you and the seniors have your usual charts up."

"We do. Would you like to see them?"

"Yes. You sometimes unearth things I don't know about."

We walked to the meeting room. Someone had taped a card over the door with the words "War Room" written in bold, black block lettering. I suspected it was Ivan's writing.

Stanton raised his eyebrows and looked at me.

"We decided to declare war on the kidnappers and the poachers. I think Gertie, in particular, likes the name. I swear I saw a glimmer in her eye when I said it the other day."

"Wouldn't surprise me. She was the toughest fifth grade teacher at the school, and I know that on a firsthand basis. You didn't mess around in her class."

Gertie had been Bill Stanton's teacher and was the only one allowed to address him as William. We entered the room and Stanton walked around reading the charts. The message board noted that Rupert didn't have any photos of the handler. However, the Succulent Saviors weren't aware there was a Caucasian involved and the others would review their photos to see if they had a picture of him.

"I would like to get one of Winslow with the poachers to clinch the connection," Stanton said.

"Do you have credit card information from the motel?"

Stanton shook his head. "Nope. He paid in cash."

"What about the car rental companies?"

Another shake of the deputy's head. "We traced the vans to the agencies by using their license plate numbers. He used fake identification."

"Have you thought about—"

Stanton interrupted me. "You'd make a terrific detective, Kelly. You're coming up with all the things we've looked into. If you ever get tired of managing this place, let's talk about a position in law enforcement."

It wasn't just a tinge of heat on my face I felt, it was burning so I knew it was red-hot blush. "Sorry."

Stanton laughed. "I was giving you a bad time. I know you're trying to help."

"I'll be sure to let you know as soon as possible if someone finds a photo."

Stanton nodded. "In case you were wondering, we know Michael can vouch for the handler's connection to the poachers, but a photo would help."

We walked back to the kitchen area, where Tommy had put out the description of his next project. He enthusiastically launched into an explanation. I went to my quarters to get ready for the day. The dress was casual, with tomorrow being the costume day. I'd be doing some wine pickups this afternoon for the Saturday event. With that in mind, I decided on sturdy walking shoes and a light blue blouse to go with my jeans and navy company fleece.

As I was about to start my Jeep, I thought of Joe and his new camera. I wondered if he had photos of the handler. I found the number of his bait shop and called.

"Hello, this is Joe," he answered.

I explained about the handler, a Caucasian man, not being caught, and asked if he thought he had any photos of him.

"As a matter of fact, I do. Mornin' before the raid, when all the activity began to increase, he was here a couple of times. Got pictures of him helpin' with the sacks. Then, when he got in his car, I used my nifty close-up button, and got a photo of him and his license plate number."

"Wow, Joe. You were on it. That's fabulous news."

"A warden is comin' by this afternoon to get my notes in case they're helpful. I was goin' to ask him if they needed the photos I have. Now I know they do, I'll send them to Warden Rodriguez."

"Please send them to me as well. I'll pass them on to Stanton and the Sentinels."

"Will do."

I gave him my email address and ended the call.

The regular lot at the center was almost full, so I parked over by the main building like I'd done the previous evening. I checked my emails and saw one from Joe with two photos attached. I forwarded them to Stanton and the group.

The fog hadn't burned off yet, and its gray blanket obscured the trees, moistened the air, and dampened the sound of people conversing as they headed for the meeting. I entered the barn. A table with beverages held a wide assortment of tempting pastries. Michael, Scott, the Sentinels, and several other people were seated on the left side of the building. In front of them was a podium with a microphone.

At the designated start time, Michael picked up the mic. "Welcome once again, everyone. I'm excited you will have an opportunity to hear what the

Redwood Cove Community Center has brought to a wide variety of people. I hope when you've heard their stories, you'll want to replicate this model."

He introduced the Silver Sentinels, not mentioning their crime-solving role. Gertie talked about several of her elderly friends who had become increasingly reclusive. The classes and the gatherings at the center had brought them out, and they were now regular attendees.

"One of them went from living on frozen dinners she'd purchase by the case to having her own plot of land here where she raises all of her vegetables. You'll have an opportunity to see that area this afternoon."

Mary, Ivan, Rudy, and the Professor each had stories to share about community changes and the impact on people and groups they knew.

The veterans spoke about having their lives turned around. Many of them had been homeless. They all were learning skills to lead them back to productive lives. Several gave examples. One announced there'd be a PTSD service dog training exhibition later in the day.

Jim Patterson, the farm manager, talked about the classes being offered. There would be mini sessions in the afternoon so guests could experience them firsthand.

He added, "I have a special treat for you right now so you can get a glimpse of the participants in one of your options."

Bruce Kincaid, the goat herder, entered through the back doors with the flock of miniature baby goats and his two working dogs. A space had been left clear of chairs. The goats bleated, milled around, then stopped and stared at the people. The dogs backed off, giving them more room but keeping them controlled. The goats began to buck and spin similar to what Sparky had done.

Speaking of Sparky, he was conspicuously absent. I wondered what mischief he was getting into.

"We have recently implemented goat yoga," Jim said. "These little ones will be part of the class today. I think you'll find them highly entertaining."

I overheard one woman say to the person next to her, "I participated in a goat yoga class once. I never laughed so hard. I'll definitely do that this afternoon."

The herder whistled to his dogs and the miniature creatures trotted their way out.

The morning continued in the same vein. Michael talked about how he went about putting the center together, including having a committee made up of local residents and an outreach person for the veterans. Scott talked about his role as overall manager.

Michael stepped back to the microphone. "The people here have shared with you what the creation of this center has meant to them. I found it fulfilling for me in a special way. I've helped many groups with donations. What's different about this is I've gotten to know these people firsthand. I've not just heard of the shift in their lives, I've seen it, and know I'm part of those changes."

He paused and people clapped.

"I encourage you to talk to today's speakers. They have much more they can tell you than their short presentations would allow. Lunch will be available in a few minutes."

Guests applauded again and rose from their chairs. The people who had spoken began to mingle with the crowd. The energetic nods and smiles from the philanthropists boded well for Michael's plan.

Scott joined me. "How do you feel it went?"

"Splendid. Look at all the enthusiasm around us."

Scott nodded. "It would certainly be wonderful if this became the start of this model growing across the country."

"I agree."

"What are you up to this afternoon?" Scott asked.

"I'm picking up wine for tomorrow. I hope to get back in time to participate in some of the activities," I replied.

"Are you staying for lunch?"

I shook my head. "No. I'll grab something to take with me."

Scott grinned. "Thanks for the s'mores lesson last night."

"You're welcome. Certainly a switch for me to be teaching you."

Memories of his flour-dusted kitchen during my apple pie lesson and images of lumpy macaroni and cheese flooded into my mind.

Trays of sandwiches were brought in, along with bowls of fruit and platters of salads. I told Scott I'd catch up with him later, put several sandwich quarters on a napkin, and left. I picked up cases from two wineries and then went on to my third and last stop, which was the Sagatinis' place. They didn't have a huge parking lot, so I parked on a far side, to leave room for guests.

I walked along a gently curving paved path toward the tasting area. Lush flowers grew along the right side of it. I stopped for a moment to gaze at a black and orange butterfly fluttering among purple and gold blossoms. The perfumed air was a far cry from what I'd experienced at the marina.

I approached a young woman at the outdoor tasting bar. "Hello. I'm Kelly Jackson, and I'm here to pick up wine for Michael Corrigan."

"I'm Jess. I'll let them know you're here."

She texted someone on her phone.

I noticed a black lab soaking up some sun on the deck and occasionally shaking his head.

Jess reached under the counter and came up with a tube of ointment. "Flies can be a problem for the dogs. This does a good job of repelling them. I'll put some on him."

A tourist van, with Vineyard and Wine Tours written on the side, pulled in, and people began to pour out of it and head to the tasting area.

"You're going to be very busy in a moment," I said. "I can apply that for you. I've done it with my horses and dogs at home."

"Thanks so much." Jess handed me the ointment. "His name is Duke."

She reached under the counter and pulled a box out and put it down. I could see the name Hercules Disposable Gloves on the side, with some clear gloves sticking out the top.

"I haven't seen any gloves like these before. I've used opaque or colored ones," I said.

"They're special order. We use them when doing certain wine classes. We didn't want to use ones that would make people think of physicians or dentists."

I put the tight-fitting plastic gloves on. They were basically invisible.

I froze.

Gloves like these could be the reason no fingerprints were found in Phil's van other than his.

Someone could've been wearing gloves like these.

With the poor quality of the video, they would be impossible to see.

Did someone from the Sagatini Winery steal the wine? Did Carlo or his son Lorenzo do it?

If so, why?

Chapter 22

Still thinking about my discovery, I took the cap off the tube of ointment and squeezed a small amount onto my fingertip. I gently rubbed it on both sides of the tips of the black lab's ears. He gazed at me with sleepy eyes and didn't bother to get up.

I put the cap back on the tube, took the gloves off, and patted his head. A few tail thumps on the deck gave me his doggie thanks. I rolled the gloves up and put them in my pocket. I wanted to get some clean ones if possible, but these would do if I couldn't make that happen.

Jess was busy pouring for the tour group at the end of the counter nearest the winery buildings and had been joined by two other employees wearing name tags.

I held up the ointment. "Do you want me to put it back under the counter?"

"That would be perfect," she replied. "Thanks for taking care of him."

"Do you mind if I take a couple of the disposable gloves? I think I know someone who would like to see them."

Deputy Stanton

She nodded. "Go ahead."

I went around the other end of the counter and put the fly salve away. I photographed the box and then took out two gloves. Tossing the used ones in a wastebasket, I stuffed the new ones in my pocket and placed the box next to the ointment.

"Hi, Kelly," Lorenzo said, "I have your wine ready for you."

Startled, I turned. Had he seen me take the gloves? He must be wondering why I was behind the counter where his employees worked. Best to address it.

"Glad to hear it. I put some ointment on Duke's ears to help Jess out when the crowd arrived and was putting it away. She said it was okay if I took a couple gloves. I think they're neat, and I like the idea of having ones that don't remind someone of a hospital. I'd like to show them to some people."

He smiled at me. "Help yourself."

I couldn't read anything in his face or tone of voice that indicated there was a problem or he was suspicious.

A young man wearing black jeans and a tan heavy twill shirt with Sagatini's written in red thread on the shoulder had a hand truck with four cases of wine on it. He wore a name badge with "Frank Mitchell" on it.

I started to walk away. "I'll bring my Jeep up closer. I didn't want to take any guest spots until you were ready to load."

Lorenzo shook his head. "Don't bother. It's easy enough to wheel it out there. However, first, I need you to sign off on it."

The workman, Frank, placed the cases on the ground and opened them. The helper was efficient, and it didn't take long for him to show me what was in the cases.

Lorenzo went to a drawer and pulled out a sheet of paper and a pen, put them on a clipboard, and put it on the counter. Next, he took out a ring of keys and slipped those into his left pocket, followed by a small pouch that went into his right pocket.

He brought the form over to where I was standing. "I wrote in the number of bottles and the names of the wines earlier. You need to sign to verify that's what you received."

I looked down at the clipboard and scribbled my name. That was when I noticed the tasseled shoes Lorenzo had on. He didn't have on a cap, but his patterned wine vest resembled the ones Phil wore. He was about the same height and weight as Phil.

My stomach turned. Was Lorenzo responsible for framing Phil?

I handed the forms to Lorenzo, willing myself to keep any thoughts from showing in my eyes.

"I'll make a copy for you. It won't take but a moment."

I almost said mailing it was fine. I wanted to get out of there. But it might tip him off I suspected something.

It was only a couple of minutes until he returned, but it seemed much longer.

The three of us wound our way down the paved path. I opened the back of my Jeep. Frank rearranged the other cases and placed the four new ones inside. He headed back to the main buildings. I started for the driver's side door.

Lorenzo stood in front of it. "I saw Phil yesterday when he put up fliers for those missing people. He wasn't looking at all well."

"He's had a rough couple of days."

Lorenzo didn't move.

"I need to be getting back," I said.

Lorenzo moved to the side. I reached for the door handle and felt a hard object stuck in my side.

"Don't make any noise. Go where I tell you to," Lorenzo said.

Fear raced through me. I grasped the handle tighter, afraid to let go.

"Turn to your right and walk next to me." He jabbed me with what felt like the tip of a gun. "Now."

My hand reluctantly slid off the handle, and I turned and walked next to him.

"There's a path on the left a short distance up. We'll take that."

He was so close I could feel the heat of his body next to mine.

"Phil and I had quite the conversation yesterday," Lorenzo said as we walked. "I told him you had mentioned you and the Silver Sentinels were helping him. He said at one point he thought he might be going crazy and had actually stolen the wine. Then you all helped him figure out it wasn't him because he didn't own any tasseled shoes."

The pressure from the object in my side never let up.

"If I had been wearing today's shoes when I talked with him, he might have figured it out himself. Fortunately, I didn't have them on yesterday. I forgot they were a clue when I put them on this morning."

I gulped. I think he'd just confessed to stealing the wine. Not a good sign. This didn't bode well for me.

Oh, Phil, what were you thinking?

His haggard face from yesterday morning came into my mind. He probably wasn't thinking. And he'd known Lorenzo for years.

Stalling might buy me some time. Maybe someone would come along and I could think of a way to escape. "Phil might have figured what out?"

"Really, Kelly, don't play me for a fool." Lorenzo's face hardened. "Phil said the biggest issue was the lack of someone else's fingerprints in his van. I saw the way you looked at those gloves, the realization on your face."

We reached a narrow, overgrown track through the weeds. Tall redwoods darkened the area on both sides.

"Turn here." He pushed his body against mine to force me to the left.

I began to tremble. "What are you planning to do with me?"

"Do with you? Who said I was going to do anything with you?" He smirked. "You wandered off and got lost and trapped in a cave."

Cave? What was he talking about?

"Or maybe you'll just disappear," he added.

In a quavering voice, I asked, "Why are you doing this?"

He just shook his head.

The wine theft wasn't worth him taking me by force. The only reason I could think of was he was involved in Eric's murder.

The tall weeds grabbed at my ankles. I tripped, and he reached over and jerked me up. We entered a clearing, and a rocky outcropping sloped upward in front of us. A weathered upright wooden door was in the center of it.

Lorenzo stepped aside and pointed, what I now knew for certain, was a gun at me. It was small, but a gun didn't need to be big to be deadly.

"I'm a good shot," he said. "And you can't outrun a bullet."

He was right.

Lorenzo took the keys out of his pocket. I saw him feel for the key slot and successfully insert the key. He unlocked the door without taking his eyes off me.

I'd hoped he'd look away, but no such luck.

He pushed down on the lever handle and pulled. The door groaned as he opened it, revealing a black hole.

"We used to store cases of wine here. I've had other reasons to use it recently, so luckily the lock is well-oiled."

Fleetingly, I wondered what the other reasons were. Had he held someone prisoner in there?

"Over here." He pointed at the opening.

My heart beat rapidly, and I began to shake.

Lorenzo raised the gun. "Move."

I stumbled toward him and looked into the black nothingness. Maybe getting shot was the better choice.

"Hand me your purse."

I'd forgotten it was even on my shoulder. With trembling hands, I passed it to him. He backed away a few steps, keeping the gun aimed at me.

"No one is getting in the way of my dream," he mumbled and dumped the purse's contents on the ground. He rummaged through the pile with quick glances in my direction, all the while keeping the gun aimed at me. Lorenzo put my phone, car keys, and Swiss Army knife off to one side.

He picked up the pouch labeled cosmetics and crammed it back into my purse. "You won't be needing this," he muttered.

He scooped up the rest of my purse paraphernalia and shoved it in after the pouch then tossed my purse into the blackness. He picked up my phone and slipped it into his left pocket. The keys and the knife went into his right one.

"You can scream and yell all you want. No one will hear you." He gestured with his gun for me to enter. "Sorry." The grin that accompanied the words held no humor. "No light bulbs."

I began to back away. "I can't. I'm claustrophobic."

He lunged toward me, grabbed my arm, and hauled me to the black mouth.

He shoved me in.

"No!" I screamed.

I pitched forward and landed hard on my knees. Pain shot through my legs. My momentum kept me going, and I ended up spread-eagle face down on the floor of the cave.

The door slammed shut.

Complete and utter darkness enveloped me.

Chapter 23

Pitch black.

My heart began to race. My breathing came in short gasps. The beginnings of a panic attack. I hadn't had one in years, but I recognized the signs. One of those wouldn't help me figure a way out. I sat up and willed myself to be calm and take deep breaths. I pulled my legs into my chest and wrapped my arms around them. Then I put my forehead on my knees. I wanted to occupy the smallest space possible, not knowing what might be around me in the dark. The cold musty air penetrated my clothes, and I shivered.

My breathing slowed but was by no means normal. I needed to find my purse. That meant I was going to need to feel my way around. I hoped Lorenzo's recent use of the cave had encouraged any crawling visitors to vacate the place.

I ventured forward on my hands and knees, patting the area in front of me, and felt sharp stabs of pain from my knees. The floor was packed dirt, chilling to the touch. A moldy smell permeated the room.

I sobbed with relief when my hand felt the leather strap. Pulling the purse to me, I sat cross-legged on the floor. What Lorenzo had mistaken for a cosmetic pouch was actually a small bag of tools I carried with me in my fanny pack when I was working on the ranch. My fashionista sister had given me the pouch, hoping to encourage me to carry makeup with me.

I'd found it more beneficial for tools. I'd transferred the pouch to my purse when I came to Redwood Cove. The assortment of items had proven useful on more than one occasion.

Today they might save my life.

I took the pouch out and unzipped it. I felt for the miniature three-inch flashlight. My fingers closed on the cylindrical object, and I pulled it out and turned it on. The beam was small but powerful. I did a short sweep of the area in front of me and saw the door.

Did I want to check behind me? See what might be lurking there? Had some animal found a way in and made the cave its lair? Or was it better not to know and concentrate on getting out?

I decided to look. Maybe I'd even see something I could use. I took a deep breath and turned around, shining the light behind me. It didn't penetrate the darkest corners, but, to my relief, no animal eyes reflected back at me. No army of bugs marched in my direction.

I sighed with a sense of being reprieved. There were several wooden barrels along one wall, but I didn't see anything that would help me escape. I turned back around and shined the light into my pouch.

The knife Lorenzo had taken was much more than a pocket knife and was my main source for tools. However, I'd created my travel pouch as backup if something happened to the knife. It contained a kit with several items in it, including a little screwdriver.

I crawled to the door and examined it. The door handle was screwed in. I put the flashlight in my mouth and began working on one of the screws. It was slow going as it was rusted. The screw hadn't received the upkeep that Lorenzo had given the lock.

My light might not last through the process. I turned it off and gasped at the return of the pitch black. I felt the start of another panic attack as my breath quickened. I focused my thoughts on turning the screwdriver, one rotation after another. A movement mantra. The screw loosened and fell to the floor.

One down!

I turned the light on, focused on another screw, and turned the light off again. My fear lessened as hope returned. Finally, the screws were all out. I pried the metal plate off the door. My light showed the locking mechanism. I tried to push it aside with the blade of the screwdriver. It didn't budge. I tried again, but nothing.

I was trapped! I began panting. A full-on panic attack had started. My heart raced. I couldn't get out. I felt frozen, unable to move.

Stop with the negative thoughts, the fear. I've been in tight situations before.

The fast breathing didn't stop, but I willed myself to move. I put the flashlight down, felt with my fingers for the mechanism, inserted the screwdriver, and used both hands to push. Still nothing. I changed my position to be able to use more of my arm. I took a deep breath and, with every bit of willpower and muscle I had, I pushed. It moved ever so slightly. Two more tries and I felt the spring release.

I opened the door a crack and looked around the clearing, blinking at the bright light. I didn't see anyone.

Shoving the door open, I fell into the patch of sunlight in front of the doorway, still panting. I lay on my back, soaking up the warmth.

I knew the attack would quit at some point. I just had to wait. But Lorenzo could return, so I needed to hide. I staggered over to a thick patch of bushes and sprawled on the ground behind them.

After a few minutes, my breathing returned to normal. I took a deep breath and stood. Other than being a little lightheaded, I felt okay. Another check around and still no sign of anyone. I returned to the cave. My flashlight was on the threshold. I picked it up, turned it on, and spotted my purse. To get it meant I needed to put a foot back into the cave.

I gave myself a count of three, put my foot in as if it were a sacrifice, leaned in, and grabbed my purse. I jerked back out of the room.

Time to get out of here. I paused for a moment and decided to try to leave the cave looking like it had when Lorenzo left. I closed the door. Nothing on the outside indicated the plate had been taken off inside. Done!

I hurried down the path.

Lorenzo was the only one I was worried about seeing me, and I figured he was long gone from this trail. As I neared the main path, I slowed. Ornamental oleanders created a dense growth on the left-hand side and provided cover for me to hide behind. I moved along next to them as I neared the main buildings. My Jeep was still there on the edge of the parking lot. I had a spare key attached under the right front fender.

The tour bus had left. Jess appeared to be washing glasses. Duke the dog was still soaking up rays. How long had I been gone? My watch said forty-five minutes. Unbelievable.

No sign of Lorenzo. Keeping low, I hoped my Jeep would block anyone from seeing me. I felt under the wheel well and found the key carrier Dad had put there. I hadn't worried about car thieves when he had put it in. They'd just break the windows. But things happened and having a spare made sense.

Retrieving the key, I entered via the passenger door and slid over to the driver's side. I started the car and did a U-turn. Just as I exited the plaza, I spotted Lorenzo running across the courtyard to the garage, throwing glances in my direction.

When I reached the highway, I wanted to turn left toward Redwood Cove but couldn't. A large tour bus blocked both lanes of the road as it navigated the sharp turn into the winery. I thought fleetingly about asking for help but didn't know what kind of chaos could ensue with Lorenzo, his gun, and a busload of people. I turned right and hit the gas. I knew the area was remote and it would be miles before I reached the next town but felt I had no choice.

The road was typical of the area, with ocean and drop-offs on my right and redwoods on my left...along with lots of curves. A plateau began to appear on my right, separating the ocean cliffs from the roadway. My rearview mirror showed Lorenzo behind me and gaining fast in a convertible sports car. I didn't dare go any faster. My car was swerving from side to side as it was. The wine cases slid back and forth, with the glass bottles crashing against each other.

Suddenly, I heard the sound of shattering glass. I looked in the mirror and saw my rear window in pieces...and Lorenzo on my tail with his gun aimed in my direction. A sign inidcated a road would soon be off to my left. If I slammed on my brakes to make a turn, I'd be that much closer to Lorenzo and his gun.

The oncoming traffic lane was empty and I could see a ways down the road. I moved into it away from Lorenzo, slammed on my brakes, and made a sharp turn. The move caught Lorenzo by surprise, and he went flying past the road I'd turned onto.

I braked to a stop. Going up an unknown road with a gunman right behind me wouldn't be a wise move. For all I knew, it came to a dead end.

I did a U-turn and prepared to hit Lorenzo's car when he turned into the road. My Jeep could do some serious damage to his small vehicle.

Lorenzo surprised me. He hadn't turned around to come back. Instead, I saw his car reversing past the entrance and saw him begin to turn toward me. This was my chance.

I hit the gas and caught his car broadside, pushing it off the edge of the road to a flat area below. I slammed on my brakes in time to not follow Lorenzo on his downward path. His car rolled over and over again, landing upright. When it came to a stop, I could see Lorenzo slumped over the wheel, held in place by his seat belt.

I backed up, parked on the shoulder, and turned on my hazard lights. I did a combination run and slide down the hill. As I approached, I could see a trickle of blood running down the side of his face as it rested on the steering wheel. Reaching him, I wrenched open the door, felt for a pulse, and found one. I spied the gun on the floor next to his feet.

Pulling one of the disposable gloves out of my pocket, I put it on, and picked up the gun. I wanted to handle it as little as possible. I noticed a big boulder to my left. I ran over to it and around the back. Tucking the weapon into a space underneath the rock, I grabbed a couple of smaller stones to cover the gun up. Removing the glove, I put it back in my pocket.

Returning to Lorenzo, I heard him groan. He wasn't getting away if I had anything to say about it. I removed the ignition keys and fought my way back up the hill. I removed a rope and a dog leash from the equipment bag in my Jeep and went back down.

Lorenzo's hands dangled down on each side of the wheel. I grabbed the right one and put it behind his back. I did the same with his left. The dog leash was slender leather, strong and supple. I did a figure eight and then a square knot.

I used the rope to bind his legs at the ankles. I made sure the finishing knot was in front and out of reach of his hands.

I thought about my phone. I shuddered at the thought of reaching into his pocket but knew it might prove valuable to have. I made a face, screwed up my courage, and searched his left pocket. I felt the phone and pulled it out. The other items could wait.

I checked and found there was no cell reception, which didn't surprise me. Once more I struggled up the hill. Reaching the Jeep, I started it up and headed back the way Lorenzo and I had come to find a place where I could make a phone call. The first place I reached was the Sagatini Winery. I hesitated but then decided it wouldn't be wise to make the call from there. I didn't know if some of the workers were in on what Lorenzo was up to and whether or not Lorenzo had said something to them about me. His father might also be part of it.

I knew there was a tasting room for another vintner a short distance ahead. A couple of minutes later I pulled into their parking lot, jumped out of my vehicle, and ran in. I was about to say there'd been an accident but realized that wasn't true. I had rammed Lorenzo off the road intentionally.

A young woman looked up as I rushed in. "A car went off the road and a man is injured. I'd like to use your phone to call nine-one-one."

"Of course. Follow me." She led me to an empty office then left.

I made my call and mentioned that a crime was involved. I wanted the police there as well as the paramedics.

I knew Stanton's number by heart from the many times I'd called him from the inn.

"Deputy Stanton," he answered.

"It's Kelly. There's a car off the road. Lorenzo Sagatini is in it. He's the wine thief, and I think he might have killed Eric."

"I just heard about the car and driver on the radio. I'm on my way. Meet me there."

"Got it."

I thanked the woman for the use of the phone and headed back to Lorenzo. I parked at the same spot and put on my flashers. As I exited the car, I heard sirens approaching and an ambulance braked to a halt behind my Jeep.

I didn't need to show them where the car was. It was clearly visible, and Lorenzo was still slumped at the wheel.

One of medics approached me as two others pulled out a stretcher and began to slide down the hill. "The phone message we received said a crime was involved."

I nodded. "That's why I tied him up before I left to make the call."

A deputy sheriff's car joined the line of vehicles. Deputy Sheriff Davidson got out.

"Stanton contacted me. He'll be here in a few minutes. You can explain to him the circumstances. I'm going to stay with the guy in the car."

He went down the hill, where the paramedics had put Lorenzo on the stretcher and were untying his hands and legs. The third paramedic joined them.

Another law enforcement vehicle arrived and made a line of four vehicles, all with lights flashing. This time it was Stanton. He gave a low whistle when he saw the back window of my Jeep. "Is that from a gunshot?"

I nodded. "Lorenzo. I took his gun out of his car and stashed it behind a rock." I reached in my pocket and took our Lorenzo's keys and handed them to Stanton. "I took these out of his sports car."

Deputy Sheriff Davidson and the three other men reached the top of the hill with their cargo, all panting slightly. The medics pulled out a gurney and transferred Lorenzo onto it. Davidson handcuffed his right arm to the bed rail.

Lorenzo's eyes opened, and he blinked a few times. He gazed around in a confused fashion. Then he spotted me and his eyes focused.

His jaw clenched. Pure hate flowed from his eyes.

I shivered at the intensity of his emotion.

"Davidson, did you find any weapons on him?" Stanton asked.

"Yes." He held up my knife.

"That's mine," I said. "Lorenzo took it from me."

"We have to enter it as evidence," Stanton said. "I'll be sure you get it back."

Davidson turned to go. "I'll follow him to the hospital."

"Okay. I'll catch up with you after Kelly tells me what happened."

The ambulance and the officer left, and Stanton and I clambered down the hill. I took him to where the gun rested underneath the rock.

I pulled out my clear disposable glove. "I had this on so as not to mess up the prints or contaminate the evidence."

Stanton took out an evidence bag, along with a latex glove from a compartment on his belt. He picked up the gun and placed the weapon in the bag. "Good thinking."

I continued to hold up the glove. "This is what started the whole event." I went over everything that had happened.

"I'm glad Phil's off the hook," Stanton said. "Too bad Lorenzo wasn't willing to tell you why he did it."

"For him to lock me up…and to do whatever else he had planned, I'm guessing it had to do with Eric Stapleton's murder. They'd been working together on the winery sale Lorenzo wanted so badly so he could begin the new venture he was passionate about."

"Makes sense," Stanton said. "I want you to show me the cave where he held you captive."

My heart plummeted at the thought of going near the blackness again. "Can I just give you directions?"

Stanton shook his head. "I'm sure what you experienced was terrifying. You don't need to go in, just take me to it."

We drove the short distance back to the winery.

Carlo Sagatini came rushing out as we parked and approached Deputy Stanton. "The hospital just called and said my son was injured. I'm on my way there now. Do you know anything about his condition?"

"He was conscious when the paramedics drove away," Stanton replied.

"Thank goodness." The elderly gentleman trotted toward the garage.

My guess was there'd be no winery sale now. That was what Lorenzo's father wanted, but I was sure not in this way.

I nodded my head toward the path. "The cave is this way."

We started down the path.

I shared with Stanton why I hadn't stopped here to make the call.

Stanton nodded. "I understand. We'll be questioning the staff and family to see if they know anything."

We took the overgrown path and then walked into the clearing. I followed Stanton but kept back several feet from the entrance to the cave. Stanton took the flashlight from his belt, opened the door, and went in. He emerged a few minutes later, grabbed the door, and went back in, closing it behind him.

My heart beat faster as I thought about that closed door, the pitch black. The smell of the mold.

Stanton emerged and gave me a pitying look. "I wanted to experience what it was like to have been in your situation. It might be useful in testimony." He shook his head. "Unpleasant, to say the least."

Unpleasant didn't start to describe it.

I figured I'd be joining Julie in the nightmare department for a while.

Chapter 24

I drove back to the inn, reflecting on what had taken place. Phil's name had been cleared. That was a tremendous relief. We still had Eric's murder to solve, but I felt we were getting close. Today wasn't a day I ever wanted to relive, but it was a successful one.

I parked and took a minute to text the Sentinels to let them know the wine thief had been caught and I'd explain later. I did a quick check in the car mirror. I didn't know if the terror I'd experienced was visible. It didn't appear to be. The knees of my jeans were dirty but not torn. I ran my fingers through my hair, got out of the Jeep, and entered the inn.

Julie and Sebastian were all smiles as they chopped and stirred in the kitchen. The room smelled of a variety of spices and had a comfort food aroma about it. Stepping back to normalcy brought light back into my life and pushed back the darkness that had gripped me.

Julie held out a bowl. "Hi, Kelly. Would you like to try some of our Wild West Chili?"

The thought of hot, healthy food perked me up. My meager lunch had vanished a while ago. "I'd love to have some."

"Need the garnish," Sebastian said with a wide grin as he sprinkled something on top of the chili. "Minced wild chickweed will do the trick. And some sourdough bread to finish it off." He placed a piece on top of the bowl.

I sat at the table and enjoyed the taste of the many ingredients. The wild edible reminded me of a mild onion. Helen had put mail on the table. I went through it as I ate then stopped when I saw one addressed to Phil in care of Redwood Cove Bed and Breakfast from Eric Stapleton. The postmark was the day he died.

I finished the chili and the last of my bread. "Delicious. I'll look forward to having more tomorrow. Thanks."

I went to my quarters with Phil's letter. Sitting on the couch, I called him.

"I have some good news." I proceeded to tell him about Lorenzo stealing the wine.

"Fantastic, Kelly. Did he give you any reason why he did it?"

"No. That's the question of the day. There's a letter addressed to you from Eric. Maybe that will shed some light on the matter. Do you want me to take it to your room?"

"No. It'll be a while before I'm back, and I'm anxious to know what it says. Please open it and read what's there to me."

I did as he asked. There was a document with numbers and percentages from the Anderson Chemical Analysis Company, along with a handwritten note from Eric.

"There's a page with a lot of numbers on it. I don't know what the figures mean. There is a note from Eric saying he wanted you to have a chance to look at the report before you two got together again and says he plans to discuss what it has to say with Lorenzo."

"I'll head back to the inn and see what it is. I can be there in about fifteen minutes."

"I'll leave the letter on the table in the kitchen."

We said our goodbyes, and I went back to the main workroom and put the information next to the other mail.

Then I headed to take a much-needed shower. The dirt and dank air from the cave, along with the exertion of climbing up and down the hill meant that was the next call to action. When I reached my quarters, I pulled my jean legs up to examine what damage had been done. There were a few scratches and I expected there'd be extensive bruising. I'd suffered worse many times when I'd been thrown from a horse.

I checked the clock and found it was only a little after three. If I put some speed on, I could still attend part of the event. It went until five. Twenty minutes later, refreshed from the shower and wearing clean clothes, I headed out my door.

Phil sat at the table reading the report.

"Is it anything important?" I asked.

Phil nodded. "I need to study it some more, but there's a good chance it's what got Eric killed."

"How so?"

"Eric sent some of Lorenzo's wine to this company to be analyzed to find out what type of grapes were present. What I'm seeing so far indicates a very cheap type of grape had been substituted to make their pinot noir instead of their usual choice. That's the wine the Sagatinis are most famous for and have the largest amount of. If this is true, that's fraud. The buyers of the winery were being lied to, as well as the customers buying their pinot noir."

"Couldn't people tell when they tasted it?"

"Not necessarily. Surprisingly, there have been similar incidents in the wine world. It went undetected in one famous winery for a couple of years. In that case, they'd been sold different grapes than what they thought they were purchasing. The grape seller was at fault. In Lorenzo's case, he sells the cheap wine at the high price of the award-winning wine and creates a nice profit."

"He must've been desperate for money to take the risk of someone discovering what he'd done."

"Wine tasting isn't the exact science that some make it out to be. When you buy an award-winning, expensive wine from a known winery, you expect it to be good. It's like commercial airline pilots who go through special training to see what's really there. The mind's eye will fill in what's missing because it expects to see that. Wine tasting is a bit like that as well. If someone did notice something, they might just think that bottle was off."

"Maybe that's why Lorenzo framed you...to get you out of the way."

Phil frowned. "Why do you say that?"

"Remember when we did the wine tasting and you thought there was something wrong with the wine? Lorenzo said maybe you were losing your ability to taste. You were going to compare it with a bottle you had at home. Maybe he was afraid you had a bottle from before he began producing the altered wine."

Phil nodded. "I forgot completely about that. If that's what he was up to, the plan worked. I doubt I would've checked on the wine when I got home."

"He mentioned your taste being off more than once, like he was trying to drive that point home."

Phil stood. "I'll contact Deputy Stanton with this news. Maybe it'll be enough to get Lorenzo to talk."

"That would be wonderful. I'm going to go see the end of the event at the community center."

As I got in the Jeep, I heard multiple text alerts from my phone. The Silver Sentinels sent their exclamations of happiness about Phil being cleared. Then I remembered the wine in the back of the car. Had it survived the wild ride?

I got out and opened the tailgate. I picked up the towel I kept in the back and swept the shattered glass from the back window off of the boxes. I checked each case. Amazingly, none of the bottles had broken.

The parking lot of the center was still full and people stood conversing in small groups. I parked and walked toward the barn. I stopped when I saw men and women on mats in the pasture on my right. A woman at the front struck a yoga pose and the others duplicated it…only with a lot of laughs added.

Goats were everywhere. One jumped on a woman's back and began nibbling her hair. She pulled her ponytail away with a giggle. A little brown and black goat touched noses with a man and gave out a loud bleat. He laughed so hard he fell forward and lost his pose. One began jumping from one back to another, making his way around the group. Why was I not surprised it was Sparky?

I continued on to the meeting area. A large chart had been put up listing activities, times, and locations. The information was in the program, but this was an easy visual. A tour of the center was about to start. Scott had given me a private tour when the place was built, but I was interested in seeing it now.

I spied Mary and Gertie near the barn, talking to two of the women guests from last night. Scott was nowhere to be seen. He was probably helping at one of the events.

Arriving at the starting point, I saw the farm manager, Jim Patterson, with a badge proclaiming him the tour leader.

"Hi, Kelly. Are you going to join us?"

"I am. It's been a while since I've walked the grounds."

"They've changed a lot. The garden is flourishing and more cabins for the veterans have been added."

"I didn't see Sparky this morning during your goat exhibition. Did he get in trouble?"

Jim arched his eyebrows and put a hand on his chest in a gesture of mock surprise. "Sparky? In trouble? Surely you jest."

I laughed. "He is a handful."

"Sparky was under house arrest. He got loose and found the vegetable garden. Fortunately, Garl nabbed him before he did much damage. We decided it was best to keep him under tight lock and key."

"Understandable."

"Incidentally, Garl's been hired as assistant farm manager. He knows animals and gardening and will be a good fit."

"I'm glad to hear he'll be staying. He seems like a nice guy."

Jim nodded. "He is."

A group of eight of us began a leisurely stroll as Jim talked about the area. As we passed the llamas, he explained their wool was used for classes. People learned how to spin it to make yarn and then dye it. From there they had an opportunity to create a variety of items like scarves and blankets.

"We're interested in starting from scratch as much as possible. People have a chance to appreciate what is involved in everything from making clothing to growing organic vegetables."

We arrived at the garden. Not one weed was to be seen among the thriving plants.

Not like the path I'd been on earlier. I shook my head to clear it of those thoughts.

"The veterans living on-site tend this portion," Jim said. "They take turns selling the produce at the local farmer's market and split the proceeds. They can use as many of the vegetables for their personal cooking as they wish. We strive to create healthy habits for everyone involved in the center."

The garden had been in its infancy when I'd last seen it. Now there were rows and rows of healthy, mature plants.

Jim pointed to an area of the garden. "Over here people who are interested are given a plot of their own. We have fifteen people signed up and are getting requests for more spaces, which we intend to provide. I help them learn how to compost and care for the plants. We plan on having seasonal classes so people can plan what they want to grow."

I noticed a small area with a name stake that read, "Medicinal." "What grows here?"

"A group of people wanted to explore herbal remedies. Plants are chosen carefully for their healing attributes." He raised his eyebrows and addressed the group. "We do not grow marijuana, which this area of the coast is known to produce."

We all chuckled and continued on under the towering redwoods, glimpses of blue sky showing through their branches. The veterans' mini log cabins were tucked in among the trees, a ways off the path for privacy. Jim explained there were ten cabins, with more under construction. Veterans wanting to learn the building trade were doing the work.

"Many of them have emotional issues to deal with. Some have PTSD. They get counseling as needed and can stay here as long as they wish. While they're here, we help them learn new skills and find jobs."

A woman with long, black hair and numerous thin gold bracelets on her wrist asked, "Have any of the veterans transitioned out yet?"

"Absolutely," Jim replied. "As you heard this morning, we have a PTSD service dog training program. One man recently joined a dog trainer in a permanent position as a result of what he learned here. Another veteran is an assistant at a woodworking school."

A man in what I thought looked like a cashmere sweater said, "It sounds like they're given opportunities to explore different skills and find ones that are a good fit."

"Exactly," Jim replied. "What might have been an interest before they joined the military, often changes. When they come back from serving, they're not always sure what they want to do with their lives. This can add additional confusion to reentering civilian life."

Jim led us to a path that had a sign reading "Meditation Garden." "We created this as a place to enhance emotional well-being. Plants with therapeutic aromas were chosen; hence you'll find lavender, dwarf cypress, and jasmine, along with numerous others."

This area had grown tremendously since I'd first seen it. Stone benches lined the paths. Secluded areas had a chair, inviting someone to sit and relax alone. Stones covered with bright green moss nestled in nooks and crannies. Here and there, piles of pebbles were arranged in various formations.

"The garden is meant to provide a place for people to rest and renew," Jim said.

Rest and renew. I needed that right now.

I touched Jim's arm. "I'm going to stay here a while. I know how to get back."

"Sure, Kelly. Stay as long as you like."

"I know this was one of the projects you were excited about. You did a magnificent job."

Jim smiled. "Thanks."

The group continued on and I found a chair in an isolated alcove. The sweet scent of lavender flowers washed over me. I filled my lungs with their perfume, imagining it pushing out the dank air I'd inhaled earlier. I hadn't realized how uptight I had been until I felt the tension start to slip away.

My thoughts wandered to Scott. I wondered if he was going to be able to live up to what he said about accepting what I did when he found out about the latest episode in my life. I remembered last night and how I had felt regarding his comments. I'd been feeling my barrier to a relationship with him going down piece by piece. It would be interesting to see his reaction when—

My phone rang, shattering the still moment.

Drat!

I wish I'd remembered to turn it off. Then I saw it was Deputy Stanton.

"Hello, Deputy Stanton."

"Hi, Kelly. I wanted you to know the new developments...especially after your ordeal today."

Kelly. He had called me by my first name. We'd agreed to a first-name basis when the Sentinels and I weren't working on a case. The only thing left on our boards was Eric's death.

"Uh...Bill, does this mean what I think it does? You know who killed Eric?"

"We do."

Chapter 25

"It was Lorenzo." Stanton continued our phone conversation. "He signed a confession...of sorts. When we read him the wine report Phil gave us, it did the trick. He swears killing Eric was an accident. They got into a shoving match over the report and Eric got caught on the edge of a table, fell backward, and hit his head on a stone counter. The blow killed him. Lorenzo put the body in Eric's truck, along with a bicycle, and drove it to where it went off the road. He got out, unloaded the bike, put the vehicle in gear, and jumped out of the way. He pedaled home."

"What explanation did he have for locking me up?" I asked.

"He said he only wanted to scare you."

Which he did.

"He wanted you to stop investigating. Claims he planned on letting you go."

I shook my head. "Yeah, right. After admitting he'd stolen the wine."

"He said the wine theft was a prank and he realized it was a mistake. He knew there'd be consequences but certainly would never kill someone over what those might be."

"And shooting at me?"

"Same excuse. Claims he could have shot you if he had wanted to. He's a world-class marksman. That might be true on a gun range, but not in a speeding sports car. He'll have trouble convincing a jury with that story."

"So, if I understood Phil correctly, Lorenzo's been making cheap wine and selling it as something else with a high price tag."

"Right. Needed the money for his real estate venture. He'd served it to a number of people and no one noticed, no one until Phil, that is. Figured he could get away with it."

"Was his father in on the scheme?" I asked.

"There's no indication of that, but we'll investigate him and the others at the winery."

I took a deep breath. "I'm happy it's over, Bill."

I enjoyed using his first name to emphasize we had all the answers we'd been looking for.

"Me, too. I'll be able to keep my date with Tommy tomorrow to help him with his project."

"See you then."

We hung up, and I rose and stretched. I leaned over a lavender plant and inhaled deeply. It was over.

Wonderful, welcome words.

Time to share the good news. I headed back to the barn to find the Sentinels. It was almost five, and people were streaming to the parking lot. The group had gathered at the door and were talking to a few last guests.

I stood off to the side and waited. The people thanked the Sentinels and headed away. The five seniors turned and looked at me and I joined them.

"Stanton knows who killed Eric. It was Lorenzo Sagatini."

There was a group sigh.

"I have a feeling you have a lot to share, my dear," the Professor said.

"I do."

"I have an idea," Gertie said. "Let's meet in the morning before the food event. We can disassemble the War Room and make it back into the Silver Sentinels' Conference Room and you can tell us about it then."

Ivan rarely appeared tired, but today was an exception with his bloodshot eyes and more noticeable wrinkles. "Tomorrow good idea."

"It's been a long day," Mary said. "We have our culprits. That's what counts."

Rudy nodded. "We decided to skip the dinner tonight and rest up for tomorrow."

The excitement had taken the edge off my tiredness, but now it returned with renewed clout as my shoulders sagged. "I agree. What time do you want to meet?"

"The event starts at noon," Mary said. "Let's plan on nine thirty and we can wear our costumes to the inn."

"I forgot about your costumes for the Wild West event. What are you all going to be?" I asked.

"Surprise tomorrow," Ivan said.

"Fair enough. See you then," I replied.

The group headed for the Professor's gold Mercedes. I did a quick scan of the barn but still saw no sign of Scott. Just as well. A good night's sleep would put me in better form to tell him what had happened.

* * * *

The next morning after Helen and I finished delivering the baskets, I saw her preparing a full breakfast of bacon and eggs, along with hash browns. A loaf of homemade bread rested on the cutting board.

"That looks like a Stanton breakfast," I commented.

Helen nodded. "I'm making some for Tommy, too. He said he wanted to eat what Bill was eating."

"Cute. I think the relationship benefits both of them."

"I do too. Bill never married, has no family nearby, and has a very demanding job. Tommy and Fred are pretty good at getting people to smile, and Bill is no exception."

The dynamic duo, as I called them, never ceased to brighten my day either.

With that thought still echoing, Tommy bounded in, along with Fred on his heels. He carried a paper bag.

"Is it okay if I put out my project now?" he asked his mom.

Helen looked a question at me.

"Sure. I don't need the space," I said.

Tommy enthusiastically began spreading colored pieces of paper, stickers, clean popsicle sticks, and a myriad of other items on the table.

"What are you making?" I asked.

"A Spanish mission like in the days of early California."

The sound of crunching gravel heralded the arrival of Deputy Stanton in a black pickup truck. He'd been over often enough he knew he didn't need to knock. He entered wearing jeans and a denim shirt.

Helen handed him a cup of coffee. "Hi, Bill. Glad you could make it today."

"Me, too."

Fred put his paws on the deputy's boots.

"Good morning, Fred." He patted the basset hound then sat at the counter.

Tommy immediately sat next to him. "Thank you for helping with my project. It's always more fun to make things when I do it with you."

Stanton blinked a couple of times. It occurred to me those were words he might never have heard spoken to him before.

Julie entered the room carrying her breakfast basket, along with several books, Rex at her side. She set the remains of her meal on the counter. "Good morning, everyone." She turned to Helen. "Those cranberry muffins were delicious. That's another recipe I'd like to have."

"I'll do a trade for the chili one," Helen replied.

"Deal." She held up the books and looked at me. "These are cookbooks. I want to take you up on your offer to make copies. I've put markers on the recipes I'd like to have."

"It just so happens our official copier is here," I said.

"That's me," Tommy said. "Miss Kelly gave me the job so I could earn some extra money."

"Tommy," Helen said, "it'll be a few minutes before breakfast is ready. Why don't you start on them now?"

"Okay." He jumped up, took the books from Julie, and ran toward the office.

Fred trotted behind him.

"How are you doing?" Stanton asked Julie.

Julie smiled. "Much better. Cooking with Sebastian helped me get back into the swing of things."

"And you?" he asked me.

"Fine. Having all the answers to our puzzles gave me some of my energy back."

As well as a feeling that all is well again.

Helen smiled at me as she put plates on the counter. When I'd gotten home yesterday, I told her everything that happened. We worked as a team, and I felt it was important to keep her in the loop. I didn't want her to find out yesterday's events from someone else.

The bacon began to sizzle. Its smell reminded me of breakfast on the ranch. Mom cooked for all the cowboys as well as the family. Each morning she made sure everyone had a full stomach. Here, I mostly ate cereal or toast, and Helen usually didn't cook a traditional breakfast. Tommy normally had things like granola, yogurt, and fruit. Thinking of my family helped bring another layer of contentment to my day.

Phil knocked on the back door and I waved him in. He put his basket next to Julie's.

"Same exceptional food as always," he said to Helen. "Morning, Deputy Stanton," he said as he turned toward us.

"Thanks for helping us with Lorenzo," Stanton said. "That report got him to confess."

"Glad to hear it, and I'm especially glad all the charges against me have been dropped."

"You'll receive a call about getting your van back." He reached into his pocket. "Kelly, before I forget, here are your knife and Jeep keys."

He placed them on the counter.

Tommy came back in with the copies and handed them to Julie.

"I put my time on the sheet next to the copy machine like you asked me to," Tommy said to me.

"Thanks. You're a very efficient worker," I said.

"Perfect timing," Helen said. "We're ready to eat."

While we'd been talking, she'd taken out the bacon and drained it on paper towels and finished making scrambled eggs. Helen, too, knew how to garnish and the eggs had what appeared to be a sprinkling of minced chives. She placed warm, sliced bread and homemade strawberry jam from Gertie on the table.

Tommy again climbed on the stool next to Stanton and watched the deputy out of the corner of his eye. The officer unfolded his napkin and put it on his lap. Tommy did exactly the same thing. Stanton sipped his coffee, Tommy his milk.

Stanton might have acquired family he didn't know about.

Julie excused herself and said she'd be back in a bit. She and Sebastian would be gathering their food and heading to the center. I went to change, knowing the Sentinels would arrive soon. My western "costume" was as before...clothes I'd worn on the ranch. I changed into new boot-cut black jeans and one of my favorite blouses with pearlescent snaps and the yoke pattern on the back. My sister had picked it out for me, saying its color would do wonders for my green eyes.

I took my cowboy boots out of the closet. Tommy had polished them as one of his jobs to earn extra money. He'd done a beautiful job, and they looked almost new. I added my belt with the large silver and gold barrel racing buckle I'd won at the Wyoming Stampede. I had been so proud of my buckskin mare, Lucy, that day.

My cowboy hat rested on a shelf in the closet. I pulled it down by the two-foot-long braided horsehair stampede string which I used to cinch the hat tight when riding. My family gave me the hat as a gift when I moved to Redwood Cove to manage the inn. My two brothers, sister, Mom and Dad, and Grandpa each contributed something to it.

As I held the hat, I thought about my family. It represented them, and it would be nice to have them with me today. I wasn't ready to put it on and face the dreaded "hat hair," as my sister called the dents created by wearing it. I slipped my head through the stampede string and let the hat dangle down my back.

Ready for the event, I returned to the kitchen. Breakfast was over, and Stanton and Tommy were sorting through project parts. A delivery truck arrived and the driver placed a box on the back deck.

Tommy jumped up. "I'll go get it."

"Get ready, you two," Helen said. "I think you're going to be deluged with a ten-year-old's over-the-top excitement."

Tommy came running back in. "It's here. It's here," he shouted. "My Furbo is here."

Stanton looked at Helen quizzically.

She opened the box with a cutter. "You'll know in a minute," she said. "Be careful, Tommy," she admonished as he began to tear out the packing paper.

The boy pulled out a box and opened it. He began unpacking an assortment of equipment at the far end of the table.

"It's so cool." Tommy held up the box so Stanton could see the photo on the side. "It's a machine that lets me watch Fred when I'm away." He put it on the table. "And I can even feed him treats with it when I'm at school." He looked at his mom. "But only during lunch."

Stanton shook his head and laughed. "Amazing. I've never heard of such a thing."

Helen came and stood next to Stanton. "It's why Tommy has been wanting to work so he could buy it. It was on sale, so I loaned him the money."

"I'm guessing we have another project to do, and the Furbo is the one we'll start with first." Stanton joined Tommy and picked up the directions sheet.

Helen surveyed the table. "With all that's here, Bill, you might be here through lunch."

"Fine with me. I have the whole day off and there's nowhere I'd rather be."

Helen blushed and began to finish the dishes.

Stanton and Tommy had their heads together as they began to assemble the machine.

The Professor's gold Mercedes rolled by the side window. He parked next to Stanton's truck. The group emerged, walked up the back steps, and paraded in.

We all stopped what we'd been doing when they entered.

Tommy's jaw dropped and his eyes widened.

The Wild West had arrived.

Chapter 26

The Professor and the group were in full regalia.

"Well, I'll be," Stanton said.

"Remember what I taught you, William. Whatever you do in life, do it as best you can," Gertie said, though it was hard to make out her face with the huge faded bonnet she had on. Strips of cloth tied in a bow secured it in place. She wore a simple, long, calico dress in hues of cream and brown.

"That's quite a hat," I said.

"It was my great grandmother's. Wore it on a wagon train across the country to get here. It's the real McCoy."

Mary had walked in behind her, wearing a tan dress with fringe along the bottom and embroidered flowers up the right side of the skirt. Gold medals covered the bodice, and she wore a wide-brimmed hat.

Then I noticed the rifle she carried.

"Don't worry, honey," she said when she saw me stare at it. "It's not loaded."

"Let me guess," I said, "Annie Oakley, right?"

"Got it. Also known as Little Miss Sure Shot."

"I love the medals," I said.

"Don't look at them closely," Mary replied. "They're mostly for competitions in gymnastics and wrestling. I got a great deal at the thrift store—fifteen of them for five dollars."

She put down the dog carrier she'd brought in and opened the top. Princess popped into view. Today she wore a fuzzy pink coat glittering with rhinestones. "Tommy's going to take care of her while we're gone," Mary said.

More work for the Furbo, I figured.

I gave a low whistle as I admired the Professor's resplendent get-up. He wore a black suit with a silver vest showing through the front and a black bowler and carried a black walking stick with an ornate silver top.

"My turn to guess," Stanton said. "Bat Masterson."

"That's correct," the Professor replied.

"Who's he?" Tommy asked.

"Was," the Professor replied. "He was a famous man in the days of the Old West. He was good friends with Wyatt Earp."

"I've heard of him," Tommy said. "We learned about him in history class."

"Masterson had many jobs, but mainly he was a lawman," the Professor said.

"Where did you get the cane?" I'd gone over to look at it more closely. The silver head sparkled in a shaft of sunlight that had found its way into the room.

"Mary found it on eBay," he replied.

Rudy looked dapper in a blue double-breasted coat, matching blue slacks, and a white cap with a blue and gold braid for a hatband. He held a pipe. "My ship's docked in town for a while. It'll be filled with redwood, then I'm on to San Francisco. I'm off to enjoy today's festivities while the lumber is loaded."

Ivan loomed over him, wearing a red wool cap and dressed in a black-and-red-checked flannel shirt. Red suspenders held up his denim trousers. He wore heavy leather work boots with toes the size of Princess's head. In case someone wasn't sure who he was portraying, he'd tucked a small axe into his belt.

"Timber was big business for the area in the eighteen hundreds," he said.

"You all look terrific," Helen commented.

Our living history lesson completed, the Sentinels headed for the conference room.

"I'll be along shortly," I said.

I'd seen Sebastian drive in and park next to Stanton's pickup and wanted to say hi to him. I waved him in when he appeared at the back window. Julie showed up and joined us.

"Good morning," I greeted him.

"Same to you." Sebastian handed Helen the bag he'd been carrying. "Here's some fresh sourdough bread for you."

"Perfect." She took it. "We'll have it for lunch."

"Then you're set," Julie said. "I put a container of the chili in the refrigerator as a thank you for letting us use your kitchen."

Sebastian headed toward the back door. "We'll get the pots of chili from the storage shed refrigerators and be on our way."

"It's early," Julie said, "but I don't know how long it'll take to set up."

"I'll see you there." I went to join the Sentinels.

As we took down the charts, I filled them in on yesterday's events.

"I'm so glad you weren't badly hurt." Mary rolled up the chart we'd created on Eric.

The others nodded in agreement.

"Time for us to have a fun day," I said, "and leave all of this behind us."

"Yah. I go remove War Room sign." Ivan left and came back with it and started to throw it away.

"Wait." Gertie went over and got it from him. "You never know when we might need it again."

I *knew* she liked that name.

Everything was packed up. We decided to keep our notes in case we had information that might be helpful to the police.

"There's an hour before the event starts," Rudy said. "Let's go see if we can help in any way."

"If not," Mary said, "we'll be part of the decorations."

They left, and I went to get my purse and jacket from my living area. When I entered the kitchen, Stanton rose and said, "There's something I want to tell you. Let's go in the conference room."

They'd gotten the Furbo working and Tommy was feeding Fred treats with it. I didn't think he noticed us leave.

When we got to the room, Stanton said, "I don't like Tommy to hear police talk. They got the handler. Caught him at the airport as he was boarding a plane."

"Nice to have that final thread taken care of."

"I agree," Stanton said.

We went back to the kitchen, and he joined Tommy.

"Do you have it all figured out?" Stanton asked Tommy.

He nodded enthusiastically and gave Fred another treat.

"Then let's start on the school project," Stanton said.

"Okay."

The two sat and began sorting through the project supplies on the table. Tommy loved learning, so I wasn't surprised he'd be willing to let go of his new toy for a while. Most kids would probably have resisted.

"I'm off," I said to Helen.

"Have fun."

"I'm sure I will."

I arrived at the center and parked in my usual spot. Several veterans stood next to the lot. They each had small black wagons similar in size and shape as the red one I used to pull around as a kid. I watched as one of them approached a car that had just parked. A man in a chef's coat got out and opened the sliding door of his van. He reached in and pulled out a huge kettle and set it in the wagon. He took out a second container, locked the car, and the two began the walk to the barn.

I knew the crowd would be larger today as Michael had invited various members of the community to attend. Law enforcement, fire fighters, and the local wardens and rangers and others received invitations as a thank you for their services. The veterans would switch gears from helping the cooks to parking cars.

I waved one of the veterans over. "I have wine for the event in the back of my Jeep."

"Okay." He quickly unloaded the cases and put them in his wagon. "I know where they want it. I'll have it there in a jiffy."

He trundled off. I decided to peek in the main building to see if Scott was there. I opened the front door and headed for the kitchen, which was usually where I found him. Sure enough, he was stirring something on the stove.

He looked up when I entered. "You're just in time to sample my Piment D'ville Delish."

"I'm sure it'll taste as good as its name is fancy."

Scott laughed. "It's a burrito filling made with a special pepper that used to only be available from France. It's our good fortune they've started growing it locally."

Michael Corrigan entered just then. "Hi, you two. That smells incredible, Scott."

"You can try some along with Kelly. I got up at dawn and made tortillas from scratch to go with it."

Dawn. Homemade tortillas.

Of course.

That was Scott.

He took down some plates, but before he could scoop any food onto them, Sebastian came in. He walked up to Michael and stood military straight in front of him. I thought he might salute.

"Sir, I have something to tell you."

"Sebastian, I've asked you to call me Michael."

Sebastian blushed a bit, and his posture relaxed.

"What's your news?" Michael asked.

"I'll be leaving. You can offer my place to another veteran."

The way he was beaming, I expected him to go into a happy dance at any moment. "Julie's boss has offered me a job as a sous chef and a cabin on the grounds in Oregon like Julie has. She can't drive right now because of her seizure so I'll take her home when your event is over."

Michael clapped him on the back. "Good news, son. I'm happy for you."

"I'll figure out how to get my truck up there once I'm settled," Sebastian said.

Corrigan shook his head. "Let me handle that. Two of the veterans can take care of your vehicle. One will drive it up with the other one following. Then they both can come back together. I'll give them some money, and they can take the trip as a mini vacation. It'll be my congratulations to you on your new start."

"Thank you so much." Sebastian shook the men's hands and then mine in his excitement. "I need to get back to help Julie."

I was thrilled for him. I also guessed there was way more to his elation than getting the job.

Scott put a bowl of his concoction, along with some warm tortillas, on the table. He added a platter of greens. "Wild miner's lettuce to stay in keeping with the theme."

We sampled Scott's burrito filling. The peppers added a smoky, sweet flavor, but he'd been careful not to make it too spicy. The tortillas had that special taste that came from being homemade. I could always tell the difference between commercially made bread and home baked. The tortillas were no different.

Michael put down his fork. "It tasted as fabulous as it smelled." He placed his napkin next to his plate. "I'm going to go to the barn. See you there."

He left and Scott said, "Kelly, I'll be serving my food at the beginning of the event, but I've arranged for one of the veterans to take over after the initial round. I'd like to go sampling with you."

"Okay," I said. "I'll do a preliminary pass and give you a report when we get together."

"That works for me."

I noticed he'd wheeled one of the handy wagons into the kitchen.

"I'll swing by and touch bases with you," I said.

He began loading his pots onto the cart. "See you in a bit."

When I reached the barn, I saw the Sentinels at various stations helping the chefs. I spotted Cassie on the far side of the room talking to a tall, attractive man, who was helping her arrange her table. His clean-shaven face and neatly cut black hair was a far cry from her bushy-headed, bearded husband. If Ian saw them together, he wouldn't like it.

The man had had his left side toward me. He turned around to pick up a bag from the floor, and I saw his right hand was in a cast.

Could it be Ian? I was stunned. He looked like a completely different man. I walked over to them. Cassie saw me coming and ran to meet me.

She gave me a hug. "I've got my Ian back." Tears filled her eyes. "And you were part of that happening."

The stranger named Ian joined us. "Kelly, what you said to me hit home in a way I hadn't felt before. That, combined with thinking I might not ever see Cassie again, changed me. Sebastian and I talked about what I could do. I met with Cassie's boss, and he offered me a job as a waiter, something I've done in the past. My hours will coincide with Cassie's, so we'll be together on our time off."

"I'm so excited," Cassie said. "We're going to have our own small business as well. Ian was a guitarist and songwriter. He's going to bring that back into his life. I'll prepare food, and we'll offer our services for private parties."

"That's marvelous, you two. I'm so happy for you. Ian, I didn't recognize you at first."

"I've told Cassie many times before I'd change. I thought a visual declaration would help."

Cassie turned and planted a kiss on his lips. "I love you, Ian."

"I love you too." He held her close.

Cupid had been busy. Sebastian was off to a new start, and it appeared these two had mended their relationship. I said goodbye and wandered off.

I wondered what the little guy with arrows had in mind next.

The different food booths were beautifully decorated. The outdoors and the west were the theme with wild edibles in vases and various cowboy paraphernalia. Flowers adorned the tables.

After the first hour, I went by Scott's area. The simple addition of a black cowboy hat had finished off his outfit of blue jeans and a white shirt. He'd found some used cowboy boots somewhere. Their leather was wrinkled but well cared for. He was what my sister would call a long, cool drink of water on a hot day.

"Hey, cowboy," I said. "It looks like it might be time for us to take that horseback ride we talked about."

The grin on his face drooped. "A hat and boots do not a rider make."

"It'll be fun." I poked him gently in the side. "I survived two cooking lessons with you. Your turn."

"We'll see."

He and another man were giving out samples when I joined them.

"Ready?" I asked.

"You bet," he replied.

Scott turned to his helper. "Thanks for taking over with the serving."

"No problem," the man replied. "Glad to do it."

Guests had arrived and the place was packed. Many of them had chosen to wear costumes, and it was fun seeing the different interpretations of people regarding the days of the Wild West. Gamblers and saloon girls wandered among the likes of Calamity Jane and Wild Bill Hickok sampling the chefs' creations.

People smiled and laughed as they made their way around tasting the vast assortment of gourmet food. Quail eggs rested in edible nests and a variety of marinated mushrooms lined silver trays. Bright purple elderberries encircled paper-thin slices of sautéed abalone. The list went on.

Scott and I strolled and sampled. I hadn't tried the large grilled shrimp on toast on my first go around and realized too late I had to put the whole piece in my mouth or the shrimp would slide off onto the floor.

Scott turned to me just as my cheeks bulged and asked, "What do you think of the event?"

I looked at him helplessly as I chewed.

He laughed. "I didn't take one of those because I wondered if they would pose a challenge to eat."

A couple more chews, and I swallowed. "Sorry. I didn't know what I was getting in to."

"No problem."

I knew I needed to tell him about yesterday before someone else did.

"Can we go outside for a few minutes? I have some things to share with you."

"Of course. Let's go to where we had the s'mores last night."

We settled ourselves in the same chairs we'd used before. The back was low enough it didn't interfere with my hat. The patrol veterans were on the fringe of the area, as were the bodyguards.

I took a deep breath and began. "I want to tell you what happened yesterday."

I shared it all. He looked somber, but I didn't see the usual frowns.

"Kelly, I told you I accept you for who you are and what you do. I meant it. It's hard for me, but that's my problem." He reached for my hand. "I'm so glad you're okay."

As he looked at me, my emotional barriers fell away. My heart beat faster, and I took in a quick breath. I realized I was willing to risk entering into a relationship with this man.

Scott stood, as did I. "Thank you for telling me. Let's go back inside." He paused for a moment and looked at me. "How about dinner tomorrow night? Just the two of us."

I didn't look away, which was my usual avoidance technique, or come up with some excuse why I couldn't go out with him. "I'd like that."

Scott smiled and linked his arm with mine. He lightly kissed me on the forehead. "It seems we have a lot to celebrate."

Cupid had indeed been busy.

It would be interesting to see what the next chapter in our lives would bring.

Chapter 23

My cell phone number and Helen's were posted inside the front door and had been given to the guests in case they needed to reach us. They also had contact information for the Ridley House. Our staffs worked together to cover for each other. One of us didn't need to be at the inn at all times.

I grabbed my fleece off the rack at the back door, along with the truck keys. Pausing for a moment, I thought about walking. It was only a short distance, and it was a lovely day.

I shook my head. I wasn't in the mood for sightseeing or enjoying the beauties of the area. Answers were what I wanted to get as quickly as possible.

There was a parking space next to the town hall. I surveyed the area where the groups were meeting and didn't see the trucks. Joey's group must not have returned yet. I did spy Priscilla holding court with Ted over by the registration booth. I joined the small crowd that had formed around them and stood next to Helen.

Priscilla still had her pink bow, and now she had matching painted pink hooves. Tommy was scratching her back. She snorted and grunted and appeared to have a big grin on her face. Her spinning tail would give the Professor's twirling pen a run for its money.

"Is it okay if I pet her, too?" Allie asked.

"Sure," Ted said. "The more the merrier, as far as Priscilla is concerned. She gets energized by all the attention."

Allie stood across from Tommy and joined in on the pig scratching.

"I like the pink manicure," I said.

Ted smiled. "It's contest day. I thought I'd give her a little something extra to prance about."

"How did you do with finding truffles?" I asked.

The wide grin on his face gave me the answer before he spoke. "Great, but let's keep it between ourselves. I don't want the others to know about them."

"No problem. I'll keep quiet."

The sound of loud engines drew my attention to the main road into town. Four large trucks drove into view, with Joey's red one in the lead. They parked a block away. I waited while the drivers and their passengers disembarked.

"Helen, I want to talk to Elise's son. I'll see you later."

Helen nodded. "Okay."

Joey hadn't bothered to clean the mud off the windshield yet. Maybe this added to the macho look. The drivers gathered around the front of his vehicle.

As I approached, I heard a lanky man exclaim, "Look at those mudders on that truck, man. Wish I could afford a set of those."

I was close enough now to see a catalog of truck equipment had their undivided attention. None of them noticed my arrival. I cleared my throat.

They glanced in my direction.

A look of annoyance passed over Joey's face. "Afternoon, Ms. Jackson. Did you come to join us for the next trip?"

"No, not this time. May I talk to you for a few minutes?"

"Sure." Joey scowled. "Seems like you've been doing a lot of talking and asking questions, from what I hear."

Elise hadn't wasted any time.

We walked over to a bus bench and sat.

"Mom called. Told me what happened." Joey shot me an angry look. "Why can't you mind your own business?"

"Your mom must have left that part out. Daniel Stevens is a good friend of mine and currently a suspect in Ned Blaine's murder. The police called him in for more questioning. His young daughter was crying up a storm this afternoon, afraid she's going to lose her father. If you could have seen her, I think you'd understand why I've involved myself in all of this."

His frown eased a bit. "Sorry to hear about your friend and his daughter, but I don't see any way I can help you."

"Tell me what you told Ned Blaine."

"Look, Mom and I are hard up for money right now. Maybe I've done a few things I shouldn't have, but I did not kill Ned Blaine...and I do have an alibi. It's just not the one I gave the police."

"What is it?"

Printed in the United States
by Baker & Taylor Publisher Services